PENGUIN  CLASSICS

BEOWULF:
A Verse Translation

Beowulf is much the most substantial of the Old English poems we have. It survives in a single manuscript of about the year 1010, but was composed generations earlier. Its story is set centuries earlier still, on the North Sea coasts from which the Angles and Saxons came to Britain. It shows the northern heroic world, a world of deep interest to its Christian audience as the world of their ancestors, presenting it with a tragic reserve. Its poetic dignity is well kept in this classic of verse translation, often broadcast and anthologized since its first publication in 1973.

MICHAEL ALEXANDER, Berry Professor of English Literature at the University of St Andrews, has published widely on modern as well as medieval poetry. Having edited *Beowulf: A Glossed Text* for the Penguin English Poets in 1995 (revised in 2000), he has now carefully revised *Beowulf: A Verse Translation*, providing a new Introduction and much fuller notes. A poet as well as translator, his first book, *The Earliest English Poems*, appeared in Penguin Classics in 1966, his most recent, *A History of English Literature* (Palgrave), in 2000.

BEOWULF

A Verse Translation

Revised edition

Translated with an Introduction and Notes by
MICHAEL ALEXANDER

PENGUIN BOOKS

PENGUIN BOOKS

Published by the Penguin Group
Penguin Books Ltd, 80 Strand, London WC2R 0RL, England
Penguin Putnam Inc., 375 Hudson Street, New York, New York 10014, USA
Penguin Books Australia Ltd, Ringwood, Victoria, Australia
Penguin Books Canada Ltd, 10 Alcorn Avenue, Toronto, Ontario, Canada M4V 3B2
Penguin Books India (P) Ltd, 11 Community Centre, Panchsheel Park, New Delhi – 110 017, India
Penguin Books (NZ) Ltd, Cnr Rosedale and Airborne Roads, Albany, Auckland, New Zealand
Penguin Books (South Africa) (Pty) Ltd, 24 Sturdee Avenue, Rosebank 2196 South Africa

Penguin Books Ltd, Registered Offices: 80 Strand, London WC2R 0RL, England

www.penguin.com

This translation first published 1973
Revised edition published 2001
3

Copyright © Michael Alexander, 1973, 2001

All rights reserved

The moral right of the translator has been asserted

Set in 11/13.75 pt PostScript Monotype Van Dijk
Typeset by Rowland Phototypesetting Ltd, Bury St Edmunds, Suffolk
Printed in England by Clays Ltd, St Ives plc

In memory of Joseph and Winifred Alexander

Contents

Acknowledgements

In preparing this second edition, I should like to acknowledge those who helped with the first – Betty Radice, who commissioned it for Penguin Classics, Arthur Cooper, Eileen McCall and friends at the University of Stirling, and also the guardians of the manuscript, then kept in the British Museum Reading Room.

M.J.A.
St Andrews 2001

Preface

This translation of *Beowulf* was first published in 1973 by Penguin Books, who had published *The Earliest English Poems* in 1966. These poetic translations from the Anglo-Saxon have been liked by poets and anthologists, by radio producers, playwrights and composers, and by many readers. Together the two volumes have sold over half a million copies. Old English poetry has become popular.

Tennyson was the first to translate a few lines of *Beowulf*, in 1830. Other writers attracted to the poem have included William Morris, J. R. R. Tolkien, W. H. Auden, Jorge Luis Borges, Richard Wilbur, Edwin Morgan, Seamus Heaney. *Beowulf* has often been edited, and has been translated hundreds of times and into many languages. Its fame is still growing: three new scholarly editions of the Old English text have been published since 1994, including the Penguin English Poets *Beowulf: A Glossed Text* in 1995, revised in 2000. The second edition of *Beowulf: A Verse Translation* brings the translation into line with that version of the Old English text.

Recent editors have made a number of small changes to the text of the original. Newly accepted readings are acknowledged in the Notes, and the phrasing of the translation has been adjusted in about forty places. There is a new and fuller Introduction. The list of Further Reading has been extended to take account of recent scholarship, and the Notes have been much amplified. The text has been reset with line numbers every ten lines. Taken together, these changes are substantial, and the result is virtually a new book. While a redrawn Map remains with the Index of Proper

Names at the end, the Introduction is now followed by the three Genealogical Tables – a rearrangement which reflects changes in understanding. *Beowulf* now seems a poem less about physical history and more about human nature and its ancestry.

Introduction

Beowulf, the first substantial work in English, has a severe artistic dignity and a penetrating understanding of human life. Deeply rewarding as literature, it also has great cultural as well as historical interest. The crucial episodes of Beowulf's life-story unfold against a historical background of epic scope. As a young man, he defends the Danes against terrible enemies. When he comes to rule his own people, he gives them a long period of peace. In old age he successfully defends them against an enemy who had destroyed their houses by fire. He dies in this action, and the narrative ends with a prophecy of the enslavement of Beowulf's people and the building on a headland of a monumental tomb for him. His adventurous life is set on the shores of southern Scandinavia and the coasts of the North Sea. The name Beowulf is not historical, and his deeds belong to legend, but they take place in a believable historical world, the world of those who ruled the coasts surrounding Denmark in the fifth and sixth centuries.

This age, towards the end of the period known as the Wandering of the Peoples, is presented as a heroic age. Beowulf is the nephew of Hygelac, king of the Geats, a people of southern Sweden. Hygelac is certainly historical: the seventh-century Gregory of Tours, and two other Latin historians, tell us that he fell in a warlike raid on some peoples living near the mouth of the Rhine in about the year 521. By 521 Angles, Saxons and Jutes had occupied parts of south-eastern Britain, but *Beowulf* does not mention Britain. The poem is set in a north Germanic world before the arrival of Christianity, but it was written – it is agreed by scholars – in England, in English, for an English Christian audience. What was its interest for that audience?

The poem's text survives in a single manuscript copy in the British Library, dated to about the year 1010. We do not know the circumstances of *Beowulf*'s composition, and its date is not agreed, but there is some reason to think that it may have reached what is substantially its present form before the year 850. It is a literary poem, but many of its techniques and much of its material originate in older oral traditions. The poem is anonymous, and likely to remain so. It is the first large poem in English – it has more than three thousand lines – yet, as we have said, these lines include no reference to Britain. What was its interest for its English hearers, some of whom had been settled in Britain for as many as ten generations? Later audiences have found it a good story, but for its first audiences it was a good story about their ancestors.

Audience and Ancestors

The first writing about these ancestors is to be found in the Latin history completed by Bede in 731: the *Historia Ecclesiastica Gentis Anglorum*, a history of the people of the Angles. A church history, it treats the English as a single people. According to Bede, the former Roman colony of Britannia was won by Germanic tribes in the later fifth century: Angles, Saxons and Jutes, coming from the coasts between Denmark and the Rhine.

> . . . from the east came
> Angles and Saxons up to these shores,
> Seeking Britain across the broad seas,

Smart for glory, those smiths of war
That overcame the Welsh, and won a homeland.[1]

That is how the *Anglo-Saxon Chronicle* entry for 937 recalled the conquest. The 'Welsh' – that is, the inhabitants of Britain – called their fifth-century conquerors Saxons, but the Saxon King Alfred of Wessex (d. 899) refers to his people as English, and his successors called their homeland *Engla-land*, the land of the English.

The successors of King Alfred in the tenth century, the first kings of a united England, claimed three kings mentioned in *Beowulf* among their ancestors. Most prominent of these forebears is Scyld. *Beowulf* opens with the coming of Scyld, founder of the dynasty of the Scyldings, rulers of the Danes. *Þæt wæs god kyning*, the poem says of Scyld. Another 'good king' mentioned in *Beowulf* is Offa, king of the continental Angles. This Offa was claimed as an ancestor by Offa, the eighth-century king of Mercia. *Beowulf* also tells of Hengest, who may be the Hengest who, according to Bede, was employed to defend Kent in 449. Hengest of Kent was a Jute, Offa of Mercia an Angle, Alfred of Wessex a Saxon. All belonged to the *gens Anglorum*, the people of the English.

Among the many names in *Beowulf* are those of ancestors of dynasties ruling in England, ancestors with whom rulers and their households felt a continuity of identity. The poem is concerned with leaders, and their conduct. It was surely composed for a court audience, and by a cleric, since clerics could write. Senior clerics were often the kinsmen or kinswomen of rulers. The poetic language of *Beowulf* is traditional and composite rather than local, but its forms are chiefly Anglian, the dialect spoken north of the river Thames. The best scholarly guess is that a written version of the poem, close to the form in which it now survives, was produced somewhere north of the Thames. A court could have heard the poem over three evenings. It will also have been read, by a small readership. Most scholars think that *Beowulf* reached mature literary form between 750 and 950. Earlier and later dates have been proposed, but linguistic and metrical tests point to a date about the year 800.[2]

The custom of dating events from the estimated date of the birth of Christ was given currency by Bede's chronology. Readers of a translation of *Beowulf* in the third millennium of the Christian era may not know Bede's dates, and might not care how one Anglo-Saxon century differed from the next. The poem's interest is not dependent on knowledge of this kind. Yet to understand *Beowulf* it is necessary to distinguish the Anglo-Saxon audience from the persons in this story set on the continent several generations earlier. The audience, despite their regard for their ancestors, knew themselves to be significantly different. Life in England may have been more settled and cultivated than the old life back home, but a more certain difference lies in the poem's Christianity. At the first crisis in the story, it is said of Danes sacrificing to idols that they were not aware of God. The author and the audience of *Beowulf* knew themselves to be in a new and a better dispensation.

Nineteenth-century enthusiasts for the Germanic past often supposed that Old English poetry would be pagan, but this is not so. The English invaders were not aware of God, unlike the Britons, but surviving verse written in English is Christian. Literacy came with Christian monks from Rome and later from Ireland who translated the gospels into English, and wrote down laws, charters and poems in English. In France, it was different: the Franks who settled the northern part of Roman Gaul were, like the Angles, a Germanic people. But the future French learned to speak a bastard Latin, and the future English did not. If the clergy wanted to reach the people, they had to put the *god spel*, the good news of Christian redemption, into English. That is why English was written; a few manuscripts in English survive from the seventh century.

Vernacular verse survives in simple manuscripts and in single copies, anonymous and untitled. Enough remains, however, to suggest that Old English literature flourished extensively, both verse and prose. Most of the 31,000 lines of verse surviving, chiefly in manuscripts from about the year 1000, are explicitly Christian – although their Christianity is not like some varieties of Christianity that flourish today.

The father of Anglo-Saxon Christianity was Pope Gregory the Great, who sent a mission to the English in 597, prompted by the discovery, recorded by Bede in a famous story, that some fair-haired Angles on sale in the slave market in Rome were pagan. Gregory's mission landed in the Jutish kingdom of Kent, and their leader, Augustine, set up his archdiocese at Canterbury. In the next generations, the rulers of the various Anglo-Saxon kingdoms were converted, the king of Northumbria by the Italian monk Paulinus in 625. His people were more lastingly evangelized by Irish missionaries originally from Iona. The Archbishop of Canterbury from 669 to 690, Theodore, a Syrian Greek monk from Tarsus, completed the organization of a well-educated Church. A few lines of verse in English survive from Theodore's day. Old English poetry combined a sophisticated Latin literacy with an ancient native tradition of oral verse composition.

This fusion of literary and oral tradition is recorded in Bede's story of Cædmon, an illiterate cowherd employed at Whitby Abbey, who in the 670s was told by 'a certain man' – an angel – to 'sing the Creation': the Creation story found in the opening chapters of Genesis, the first book of the Bible. The English words of Cædmon's *Hymn* are added to two early manuscripts of Bede's Latin *History*, one now in St Petersburg. Cædmon, Bede goes on to say, composed several verse paraphrases of Old Testament stories told him by the monks. Such narratives are represented in the poems *Genesis*, *Exodus* and *Judith*. Two thirds of Old English poems are not biblical, but one other early poem may date from Bede's day. Early in the eighth century, a cross standing six metres high was erected at Ruthwell, near Dumfries. On the stone of this cross are carved lines from the poem known as *The Dream of the Rood*, one of the best Christian poems in the English language. *Beowulf* is the best-known Old English poem, but there are good short poems, such as *The Seafarer* and *The Wanderer*, together with poems of separated lovers, of heroism, of wisdom, of liturgical devotion, and also – in the Riddles – of diversion. Compared with other narrative verse, *Beowulf* is richer and more elevated in style. As an epic, it is of the same family as Homer's *Iliad* and *Odyssey* of the eighth century BC. More condensed and more elegiac in tone than Homer's poems, it has been thought closer in kind to Virgil's *Æneid*, of the first century BC. *Beowulf* shows Old English poetic style and versification at their best. Like other English verse it went underground in England after 1066, for with the Norman Conquest English lost its audience at court. The new rulers spoke French. Posterity was postponed.[3]

Publication and Reception

The text of *Beowulf* survives in one manuscript, now in the British Library. Forty-one lines were transcribed in 1705, and another forty-one published in the second edition of Sharon Turner's *History of the Anglo-Saxons* in 1807. The text was first published by an Icelander, Thorkelin, in Copenhagen in 1815, with a Latin translation. In 1820 it was translated by the poet Gruntvig into Danish. In 1830 a Cambridge undergraduate called Tennyson translated into his notebook a few lines, in which Beowulf 'his word-hoard unlocked'. In 1833 Tennyson's friend J. M. Kemble published the first full English edition, with a translation in

1835–7, unlocking the word-hoard for English readers. Since then *Beowulf* has been edited and translated with astonishing frequency. There have been twenty-six learned editions of the text, some revised and reissued several times. Three new British editions appeared between 1994 and 1998. Seventy complete or substantial translations of *Beowulf* into modern English have been published. There have been literally hundreds of translations altogether. These include translations into twenty-two modern languages, eight of them, at the last count, into Japanese. The poet William Morris translated the poem in 1896. Among the poets who have since rendered *Beowulf* into modern English verse are Edwin Morgan and Seamus Heaney. Tennyson and Ezra Pound translated other poems. Indeed, Anglo-Saxon verse in general has had an unacknowledged impact on modern English verse. Others indebted to it are Longfellow, Hopkins, W. H. Auden, Richard Wilbur and Geoffrey Hill.[4]

If poets have been drawn to *Beowulf*, to scholars it has proved irresistible. It is said that more learned articles have now been written about *Beowulf* than about *Hamlet*. Of these two works set in medieval Denmark, the play can be expected to remain more popular. Yet the dissemination of *Beowulf* through university study, and of its story through translation, retelling and adaptation to modern media, extends beyond English-speaking countries and beyond Europe. It was much admired by the Argentinian writer Jorge Luis Borges. It has been Gothicized for novels, plays and science fiction, and cannibalized for films such as *Clash of the Titans* (MGM, 1981). It became in 1955 a Brazilian comic-book, *O Monstro di Caim*, 'The Monster of Cain'. As for the cloud of learned articles, the brightest is '*Beowulf*: the Monsters and the Critics' (1937), by J. R. R. Tolkien, author of the immensely popular children's stories *The Hobbit* and *The Lord of the Rings*, both of which borrow much from *Beowulf*. The present verse translation, first published in 1973, has often been reprinted and anthologized. It has twice been dramatized, twice broadcast on BBC radio and once by the Australian Broadcasting Commission, turned into an audio book, and used as the basis of a one-man recited version, which has itself been published as an illustrated book and is extracted on a looped tape that can be played at the British Library. *Beowulf* enjoys an increasingly vigorous afterlife which is multiform and international.

There was an academic moment when its splendid isolation at the beginning of our literature began to prove a mixed blessing. For decades *Beowulf* stood in the entrance hall of historical courses in English Language and Literature until it became rather dusty. J. R. Clark Hall's scholarly English prose translation of 1901, revised in 1940 by C. L. Wrenn and with a preface by J. R. R. Tolkien, 'was still the "crib of choice" in Oxford in the 1960s'.[5] The crib, assisted by the gobbet, tested student resolve, and took attention away from the verse. Yet most who went on to modern literature were grateful that they had had to study Old English poetry – and this is still the case.

Approaches to the literature and history of Anglo-Saxon England are now less dry, but its world remains remote. The Norman Conquest and the profound changes in Western European attitudes that began in the twelfth century put Old English below the horizon. *Beowulf* has revived, but readers wrestle with unfamiliar names, whose bearers wrestle with trolls. The unfamiliarity wears off: the name Hrothgar is Rodger or Roger or Hodge. Hodge was the familiar name later given to the archetypal English rustic, and also to Dr Johnson's cat. Anglo-Saxon remoteness is less chronological than ideological, thanks to prejudices created by Reformation, Renaissance and Enlightenment propaganda. To Edward Gibbon, author of *The Decline and Fall of the Roman Empire* (1776–88), the Middle Ages between the Fall of Rome and the

Renaissance were a thousand years of ignorance and superstition. Dark Ages followed the Fall of Rome, when the Empire was overrun by the Goths who gave their name to the age, and by Vandals. A king of the Goths is mentioned in *Beowulf*, as is a prince of the Vandals. The Angles and Saxons were neighbours to the Vandals. As knowledge increased, prejudices changed, and the remoter past was investigated with curiosity and sympathy.

The Poem

The time has come to look at what sort of poem *Beowulf* is, as far as translation allows. In a speech before he dies, Beowulf looks to his funeral.

> 'Bid men of battle build me a tomb
> fair after fire, on the foreland by the sea
> that shall stand as a reminder of me to my people,
> towering high above Hronesness
> so that ocean travellers shall afterwards name it
> Beowulf's barrow, bending in the distance
> their masted ships through the mists upon the sea.'   (2799–805)

A barrow is a chambered tomb inside a high earthen mound. Like the tomb he orders, Beowulf's poem stands, massive, elaborate and conspicuous, above a period of which we know little. At the conclusion of the poem, as the twelve Geat warriors ride round the barrow, they utter their lament for their lord.

> Then the warriors rode around the barrow,
> twelve of them in all, athelings' sons.
> They recited a dirge to declare their grief,

>   spoke of the man, mourned their King.
>   They praised his manhood and the prowess of his hands,
>   they raised his name; it is right a man
>   should be lavish in honouring his lord and friend,
>   should love him in his heart when the leading-forth
>   from the house of flesh befalls him at last.
>
>   This was the manner of the mourning of the men of the Geats,
>   sharers in the feast, at the fall of their lord:
>   they said that he was of all the world's kings
>   the gentlest of men, and the most gracious,
>   the kindest to his people, the keenest for fame.

This funeral is like those of heroes in Homer and Virgil, and the
poem's last word is *lof-geornost*, 'most eager for renown'. This
desire for 'a name that shall never die beneath the heavens', for a
personal immortality, is the heroic motive. When he is at the
mercy of Grendel's mother, or of the dragon, Beowulf thinks of his
glory; he is *mærtha gemyndig*, 'mindful of glorious deeds'. This is
the primary theme of heroic poetry: the prowess, strength and
courage of a single man, undismayed and undefeated in the face of
all adversaries and in all adventures. As he surpasses other men,
his moment of excelling, his *aristeia*, is rewarded by fame, the
ultimate of human achievement in a heroic age. Though he must
die, his glory lives on.

   Beowulf is a heroic poem in the simple sense that it celebrates
the actions of its protagonist. Beowulf, son of Edgetheow, is the
type of a hero in that it is his eagerness to seek out and meet every
challenge alone and unarmed that makes him glorious in life and
brings him to his tragic death. He also has a hero's delight in his
own prowess, and magnanimity to lesser men. *Beowulf* is typical of
heroic poetry not only in its central figure but also in its world

and in its values. The warriors are either feasting or fighting, they are devoted to glee in hall or glory in the field, and their possessions are gold cups or gold armour, the outward and visible signs of that glee and glory. This society is such as the Greek poet Hesiod of the eighth century BC describes in his account of the age of the heroes, which intervened between the ages of bronze and iron:

> A godlike race of heroes, who are called
> The demi-gods – the race before our own.
> Foul wars and dreadful battles ruined some;
> Some sought the flocks of Oedipus, and died
> In Cadmus' land, at seven-gated Thebes;
> And some, who crossed the open sea in ships,
> For fair-haired Helen's sake, were killed at Troy.
> These men were covered up in death,
> but Zeus the son of Kronos gave the others life
> And homes apart from mortals, at Earth's edge.
> And there they live a carefree life, beside
> The whirling Ocean, on the Blessed Isles.[6]

The society of the heroic age represented in many literatures centres on a lord who in peace and war is the 'shepherd of his people', *folces hyrde* (Homer's *poimeen laōn*). He gives them shelter, food and drink in his hall; he is their ring-giver and gold-friend in peace and their shield and helmet in war. The warriors earn their mead and their armour by their courage and loyalty in war. Ideally, there is solidarity between king and *folc*.

Beowulf's last word, 'keenest for fame', spoken over the ashes by the riders on horseback, is preceded by terms less expected. It is not said of heroes such as Achilles, nor even of Aeneas, that they were gentle, gracious and kind to their people. Beowulf exemplifies the heroic ideal in a socially responsible form. The Germanic social ethic ranked the mutual obligations of lord and man above those of kinship. Beowulf's epitaph has three parts service to one part glory.

Such an ending makes it clear that *Beowulf* is more than an adventure story. In 1961 Rosemary Sutcliff successfully retold *Beowulf* for children, calling her prose tale *Dragon Slayer*. It is true that Beowulf began by fighting monsters and ends slaying a dragon. But the poem is more than an adventure full of exciting action. It is not puerile. Nor is it the product of what used to be called 'the childhood of the race'. *Dragon Slayer* omits the history of three dynasties, which frames the hero's adventurous life. The poem is (like *Hamlet*) complex, tragic, full of speeches, often reflective. The poem's centre of gravity is its desire to make out the sense of life in the heroic age. Like other early English poems, it scrutinizes human experience for any wisdom it might yield.

Except in the cruder medieval romances, heroic stories are complicated and tested by a clash of loyalties. Northern heroic tales involve a conflict between the obligation to lord or kinsman and obligations to an ally, a spouse, a host or a guest. These themes are raised in *Beowulf*, usually in the interrelated set of stories framing the central action; such stories are often alluded to rather than related fully. There is a contrast between the fullness of epic narration in the central action and the laconic ellipses in which the poem alludes to other well-known tales from northern story. This cluster of outer episodes sets the story of Beowulf's life in a much larger ethical context. The development of the foreground story is clear and simple; the episodes are arranged around and behind it, and lend a depth and complexity to the whole. In the simplest of them, Beowulf is compared to Sigemund, the greatest of dragon-slayers, and contrasted favourably with the violent Heremod. In the most complex of them we learn of the series of conflicts between Beowulf's people, the Geats, and the Swedes.

These Swedish wars are expressed in terms of a blood feud between the two royal houses over three generations. The blood feuds between the Danes and the Heathobards, and again between the Danes and the Frisians, make two more episodes: both are stories of how a marriage alliance fails to heal an ancient hatred. Two other episodes deal with murder within the kindred: one tells of an accidental fratricide, leading to a father dying of grief; the other foreshadows the deliberate treachery of Hrothgar's nephew Hrothulf.

Most of these episodes occur in the second half of the poem when Beowulf is back at home in Geatland, where they add up to a history of the Geat royal house, the Scylfing dynasty. A crucial event in this history is the death of Beowulf's lord Hygelac in a raid on peoples living at the mouth of the Rhine, the north-west corner of the Merovingian Empire, an event four times mentioned in the poem. A messenger at the end of the poem foretells that the Merovingian Franks, or the Swedes, will descend upon the Geats now that Beowulf is dead. It can be seen, even from this brief summary of the principal episodes, that vengeance, the law of the feud, governs most of the stories behind the central action. The foreground story itself is successful but not serene. Beowulf's life of away wins ends in a home defeat. We have been prepared for this by the age of the hero as he approaches his last fight, by the funeral of Scyld Shefing that opens the poem, and by the knowledge that Sigemund, Beowulf's equal, dies in his last dragon-fight 'under the grey rock' – a phrase used in setting the scene of Beowulf's last fight. There is a feeling of inevitability as Beowulf goes down before the dragon's third attack. Everything in the poem seems to have foretold this end, and the mythic pattern of the poem requires it. For *Beowulf* is not only a heroic poem and an epic, it is also a myth. Much of its power comes from the mythical level.

'Myth' is a word which has been used to mean many things,

from embodied truth to exploded fiction. Here it is taken to mean a quasi-religious story dealing with fundamentals, the kind of story which has a representative value and a satisfying or explanatory power. Legend is halfway between myth and recorded factual history. Unlike his uncle Hygelac, Beowulf is not a historical person. The name is not found in genealogies, and does not alliterate with his father's. No wife is named for Beowulf, who laments that he has no son. Names are sometimes indicative: Grendel grinds. A common noun meaning warrior is *beorn*, modern Swedish Bjorn, originally meaning Bear. Warriors are sometimes named after fierce animals. Hengest meant Stallion. The poem *Deor* concerns a nomadic minstrel; *deor* meant 'wild animal, deer'. In *Beowulf*, Hrothgar names his great hall Heorot (= Hart, Stag). Beowulf (or Biowulf, as his name is spelt in the second half of the manuscript) is a name usually derived from Bee + Wolf, large wild animal to do with bees.

Beowulf is very like a bear. He has the strength of thirty in his hands, and chooses to fight Grendel unarmed. Grendel tears himself away from this wrestling match, leaving his hand and arm behind. The only named man whom Beowulf kills in the poem is Dayraven, slayer of Hygelac, Beowulf's lord and uncle. Beowulf crushes him to death with his bare hands. He also swims under water for a superhuman length of time. Supernature is not reserved to the hero and his monster opponents. The poem's overture, the arrival of Scyld, founder of the Danes, is clearly mythical. There are traces in the central story of Beowulf as a shaman exorcizing evil spirits in alien regions. His fights are at night or in a hellish underwater region, where he receives help from God, or at the mouth of a barrow. The triple pattern of the fights is also a feature of magic and of folk-poetry. This is not to say that *Beowulf* is a fairy-tale, but that features of the hero derive from folklore, especially those features that have to do with his fights against the monsters.

Epic

Some nineteenth-century scholars liked to find the lays and folk-tales behind the text. This left W. P. Ker, a humanist scholar of northern literature, free to admire the poem's picture of the noble life but to condemn a serious hero's involvement with the bogies of folk- or fairy-tale. In 1936, J. R. R. Tolkien reunited the poem and put the monsters back at its centre, symbolic rather than allegorical. Subsequent criticism has built on Tolkien while modifying his emphases.[7]

Beowulf is a rather condensed epic poem. The epic genre resolves these questions of centre and periphery, of nature and supernature. The epic genre accommodates the mythic and the monstrous. Epic takes in all of life, representing it with an archaic truth. Such poems show war and peace, men and gods, life and death as a connected reality. The presentation is not partisan. In the *Iliad*, 'the fall of an enemy, no less than of a friend or leader, is tragic and not comic'.[8] In his analysis in the *Poetics*, Aristotle makes the action, the story itself, central. The completion of a cycle of action by the successful return of Odysseus, or by Achilles' yielding of the body of Hector to Priam, is not explained. The story carries the meaning. *Beowulf* is not merely a poem about a hero, it has the epic qualities of inclusive scope, objective treatment, unity of ethos and significant action. The poem begins with the miraculous arrival of the hero Scyld and the founding of the Scylding dynasty and of the Danish people. It ends with the death of the hero Beowulf and the imminent destruction of the Geatish people. It shows the life-cycle of a hero in Beowulf and of a people in the Danes and the Geats. Human society is at peace in Heorot and at war in Sweden and Frisia. Hrothgar's hall, Heorot, is the scene of the sharing of food, drink and gold, and the home of all that is stable and venerable in human life and society – order, custom, compliment, ceremony, feasting, poetry, laughter, and the giving and receiving of treasure and vows. The opening of the hall is celebrated by the song of a poet who tells of the Creation:

> . . . there was the music of the harp,
> the clear song of the poet, perfect in his telling
> of the remote first making of man's race.
> He told how, long ago, the Lord formed Earth,
> a plain bright to look on, locked in ocean,
> exulting established the sun and the moon
> as lights to illumine the land-dwellers
> and furnished forth the face of Earth
> with limbs and leaves. Life He then granted
> to each kind of creature that creeps and moves.   (88–97)

This recital makes it clear that Heorot is a human microcosm of the divine creation of the world, called in Old English the *middan-yeard*. Of Heorot we are told that 'its radiance lighted the lands of the world'. It is a precinct of peace, the scene of the activities which affirm peaceful values. As for war, apart from defensive war, there are feuds between kindreds and, in the cases of Unferth, Hrothulf and Hathkin, within a kindred. Not to mention the monsters. As for 'men and gods', *Beowulf* does not confine its cosmos to the human. The 'careless life' of the Danes within Heorot (like that of humanity in Eden) continues *oth thæt an ongan/ fyrene fremman, feond on helle* – 'until One began/to encompass evil, an enemy from hell'. This is so phrased as to recall Satan's intervention in Genesis. In *Beowulf*, the evil is given an origin:

> *Grendel* they called this cruel spirit,
> the fell and fen his fastness was,

the march his haunt. This unhappy being
had long lived in the land of monsters
since the Creator cast them out
as kindred of *Cain*. For that killing of Abel
the eternal Lord took vengeance.
There was no joy of that feud: far from mankind
God drove him out for his deed of shame!
From Cain came down all kinds misbegotten
– ogres and elves and evil shades –
as also the Giants, who joined in long
wars with God. He gave them their reward.   (101–13)

Grendel's immediate father is not mentioned; but Hrothgar later warns Beowulf against complacency in prosperity: 'Too close is the slayer/who shoots the wicked shaft from his bow.' This soul-slayer seems to be the Devil, mentioned in the poem at line 176. God is invoked at crucial points of the action, particularly the fights against Grendel and his mother, who are, as the poem says again and again, the descendants of Cain, the first-born human being, a fratricide. So the monsters are human: they are us. The significance of the dragon is less clear, as is the extent to which it embodies evil. But the world of men is set in a cosmic time scale from the Creation to the end of human societies, and in a mythological and perhaps sacred scale of being and of moral value.

Human history also lends scale and scope to *Beowulf*: the rise and fall of both Danish and Geatish races, the history of the Swedes over three generations, with part of that of the Heathobards, Frisians and Franks. This is the world of the Baltic and North Seas in the centuries ending the Age of Migration. History is supplemented by legend with the figures of Eormenric, Sigemund, the Brisings and Wayland. Representation is selective; the thief of the cup from the dragon's hoard is the only slave mentioned, and all speakers and chief actors, except perhaps for the coastguards, are lords, ladies or noble retainers. The mode is symbolic: the life of the people, of mankind itself, is involved in the fight of the hero-king with the dragon. The poem represents the human cost of war chiefly through women, who figure largely – as queens, wives, diplomatic hostesses; as brides, the agents or victims of marital alliances; and as widows.

A second mark of epic is objectivity. As the Grendel-kin partake of the demonic and the bestial as well as the human, their fall cannot be tragic. But each of the many individual deaths in the poem is given its space: the death of Beowulf himself has a full tragic cadence (two dying speeches, two epitaphs, a pyre and a barrow), and funerals and laments wind in and out of the story. Death, irrespective of nationality, importance or merit, is accorded due respect. Scyld, Hnæf, Ashhere, Hrethel, the 'last survivor', the hanged man's father, Hygelac and Beowulf are the most illustrious dead, but the deaths in battle of Geat enemies like Dayraven and Ongentheow are also faithfully recorded, as is the mad end of Heremod. The deaths of Sigemund and Hrothgar are notable in their omission. *Beowulf* is good at death, like Tolstoy and Homer.

The chronicler of these events is, however, less impersonal than Homer, of whom Aristotle said that he 'leaves the stage to his personages'. In *Beowulf* the world-view of oral epic is inflected by a more literary and learned perspective. A reporter of what 'we have learned' or of what he had heard, the poet also comments; and not all his comments are unexceptionable saws – they sometimes take the tone of a homily, and lines such as 182–7 can seem intrusive. More typical of the poet's exposition is the ancestry provided for Grendel, already cited. Also from Genesis are the Giants, whom God 'gave their reward', as the poet reminds us.

The poet's involvement deepens moral perspective, so that his story becomes – like the tale recited by King Hrothgar – *soth ond sarlic*, 'true and grievous'.

Much of this 'truth' comes from traditional presentation. The heroic life is crystallized into generic scenes: voyage, welcome, feast, boast, arming, fight, reward. The exchanges of speeches, or of blows, are practised, stylized. The way Beowulf negotiates his admission to Denmark and to Hrothgar's presence is a good example of how presentation is standardized and heightened. It is easier to pass over the equally traditional quality of lines like those recording the death of Grendel's mother: 'She fell to the ground;/ the sword was gory; he was glad at the deed' (1567–8). Here the sword is an agent, like the man and the monster. The detachment from the merely human viewpoint, the standing back and allowing us to see the incident as a tableau in time and space, is characteristic of epic. The familiar nuts and bolts of life are presented in elevated but simple form. Identities are preserved by rich sets of names, such as those attached to God, to kings, to ships and to armour. Values are constant: sunlight is good, cold is ominous. This is not 'imagery' but reality. The blood of Grendel's mother

> made the sword dwindle into deadly icicles;
> the war-tool wasted away. It was wonderful indeed
> how it melted away entirely, as the ice does in the spring
> when the Father unfastens the frost's grip,
> unwinds the water's ropes – He who watches over
> the times and the seasons; He is the true God.   (1605–10)

If names and values are crystallized in epic formulae, so are transitions: death is presented as sleeping, as leaving life's feast, as turning away from the courts of men, as choosing one's bed of slaughter or choosing God's light. The scene on which human life is lived is simple and consistent. Men are *hæleth under heofenum*, 'heroes beneath the heavens', *be twǽm seonum*, 'between two seas', *on middanyeard*, 'on middle-earth', *swa hit wæter bebugeth*, 'as water surrounds it'. When Beowulf enters Hrothgar's hall, his advancing footsteps boom. The sparks of Beowulf's combat with the dragon 'blaze into the distance'. The watchmen see the boats from afar; Heorot is seen from afar; Beowulf's barrow is seen from afar. Like the 'well-known headlands' of Geatland, the chief realities of the poem heave into view as and when we expect them to. This sense of a known universe is temporal as well as spatial. The coming of day or night or the seasons is regular. We know where every man comes from. Men are *niththa bearn*, 'the children of men'; tribes likewise. A man is identified as someone's son or of someone's kin; a woman is someone's daughter. For important people or swords, genealogies or lists of owners are given. Feuds are caused by specific acts. Consequences are no less important than precedences: ends or fates are given or foreshadowed. If races begin, they also end, and the speeches of the 'last survivor' of the race which left the gold of the dragon's hoard and of the messenger who brings the news of Beowulf's death show that peoples, like heroes, have finite histories. Each action in *Beowulf* has its fullness, and is set in the envelope of space and time. The ethical universe of the poem is also set in its operations of cause and consequence, origin and end. Evil and good are also strongly, if not always simply, differentiated, as in Wiglaf's speech upbraiding the cowards who did not come to Beowulf's aid.

To see nature as the scene upon which human life is lived may undervalue nature and overvalue human agency. We are told, at the end of the description of Beowulf's funeral pyre, that 'Heaven swallowed the smoke'; Heaven is an agent. In epic, human and non-human actions are part of a larger process, the authority of which is not questioned. Some readers of *Beowulf* may feel that the hand of God, and the poet pointing to it, are too visible for us to regard the cosmic process as impersonal. 'The Almighty Lord / has ruled the affairs of the race of men / thus from the beginning,' the poet tells us. But there is also much reference in the poem to the power of *wyrd*, a shaping power of fate, sometimes personal, sometimes impersonal. God, for example, does not prevent those who left the gold in the ground from cursing the man who should disturb it. At certain points the poet's bias in favour of some characters (and his horror at Grendel's crimes) is felt. But the poet, though he shapes his story and orchestrates its thematic drift, treats traditional materials with respect.

A third epic characteristic is unity of consciousness, a sense of solidarity with the universe and with the audience. Respect is felt towards the inscrutable; as where it is said of the funeral ship that moves out to sea with the body and trappings of Scyld: 'Men under heaven's/shifting skies, though skilled in counsel,/cannot say surely who unshipped that cargo.' Some respect is accorded to Grendel (although Beowulf does not 'count his continued existence/of the least use to anyone') and to the motives of the slave who stole the dragon's cup, and likewise to the reasons for the attacks by Grendel's mother and by the dragon. Life in all its forms is accepted. A public poet does not interpret life very differently from his audience; and if the *Beowulf*-poet was a literate Anglian nobleman or a scholarly cleric, he inherited his medium. The system of epic formulations perpetuates accustomed interpretations. A verbal formula crystallizes an aspect of experience, and the formulaic system might be likened to a polyhedron, a many-faceted lens, through which we see the world, schematically but coherently. Yet this communal view rarely seems primitive. The sensibility through which our *Beowulf* is presented is not merely a reflex of the world it discloses; heroic poetry is not composed by heroes. The poet admires, idealizes, identifies with, the epic synthesis and works in its conventions; but is more reflective. The *Beowulf*-poet looks back across the North Sea and knows the world has changed: the Danes, for example, carry out pagan sacrifices. 'Such was their practice,/a heathen hope', he notes, and explains that:

> the Maker was unknown to them,
> the Judge of all actions, the Almighty was unheard of,
> they knew not how to praise the Prince of Heaven,
> the Wielder of Glory.   (179–82)

Unlike his heroes, the poet is a Christian, and the cosmology is largely Christian. An Anglo-Saxon moralist, his gnomic gravity is modified in places by a Christian spiritual concern such as we find in the homilies of the time. He gives *Beowulf* a sober and often sombre tone. If he laments the passing of spirited martial ancestors, he also has a horror of war such as might be felt in a settled community in an insecure age. Education contributes a conscious eloquence and fullness to the epic style which may come from an acquaintance with Latin rhetoric. But if the *Beowulf*-poet, in making the story into the poem that it is, has deepened it, shaped it and softened it, his consciousness still operates naturally in the categories and procedures of the epic tradition. The significance and weight of *Beowulf* lie in the logic of the story and the richness of the style as much as in the commentary. The moral perspective and an almost Virgilian quality in some of the sentiment are at least partly produced by Christian retrospect. To a literate Christian consciousness, the heroic world of these heathen ancestors must have seemed doubly admirable and the limitations of heroic life doubly tragic. Soon after Anglo-Saxon rulers were converted, they sent missions to convert their continental cousins.

A fourth characteristic of epic is that the story should have a kind of self-evident and axiomatic significance. The main story of *Beowulf* is of a hero who braves two life-or-death ordeals against monsters who had killed all previous opponents and dies in a third encounter with a dragon, which he also kills. The three fights are encounters with death in different shapes (as is the earlier monster-fight in the swimming-match with Breca) and in strange, extreme situations where the hero is out of his natural element. The theme of the hero's life-story is the human challenge to death, and its glorious and tragic potentialities. It is clear why we may respond to Beowulf's challenge to the dragon:

> Passion filled the prince of the Geats:
> he allowed a cry to utter from his breast,
> roared from his stout heart: as the horn clear in battle
> his voice re-echoed through the vault of grey stone.
> The hoard-guard recognized a human voice,
> and there was no more time for talk of friendship:
> hatred stirred. Straightaway
> the breath of the dragon billowed from the rock
> in a hissing gust; the ground boomed.   (2547–55)

Much of the power of *Beowulf* comes from the elemental quality of such episodes as Scyld's coming and going, the Grendel-fight, the dive into the Mere, and the death and funeral of Beowulf. Man against death is a prominent aspect of this tale of a man who defeats two monsters and dies in killing a third. It should also be recognized that the early introduction of the Genesis framework – Creation, Cain and the Giants – universalizes the theme, so that the hero is to be seen as defending mankind against its enemies. The action moves in cycles. Hrothgar feasting in Heorot shows society working well, but this is replaced by Grendel feasting in the hall. Beowulf expels Grendel, restoring society. Then Grendel's mother attacks the hall, but Beowulf kills her and extirpates the monsters. Later, the dragon destroys Beowulf's hall, Beowulf and the dragon kill each other, and society faces destruction.

Ethos

From such an account it might seem that heroic society fails because others will not fight for Beowulf as he fought for them. In his previous encounters – fights with men and with monsters – he defends a lord and the lord's people, giving his service. In his last fight, he is protector of his people, but they will not fight for him. Had Wiglaf not helped him, Beowulf would have died without having killed the dragon. Wiglaf produces a resolution: both monster and hero are killed. But the society of the Geats now faces destruction. Heroic society depends upon the honouring of mutual obligations between lord and thane. As Wiglaf points out to the eleven cowards, the lord distributes mead and arms in peace, and in return the sharers in the feast should share in the fight. If obligation is not honoured, then, as Wiglaf puts it to the cowards: 'Death is better/for any earl than an existence of disgrace.'

Beowulf stresses mutual obligation more than individual glory: 'The bonds of kinship/nothing may remove for a man who thinks rightly.' A hero may be a godlike representative of humanity: the Christ of the Anglo-Saxon poem *The Dream of the Rood* is a *geong hæleth*, a young hero 'who would set free mankind'.⁹ Unless the hero is the champion of others, however, mere heroism is irresponsible. The brilliant Achilles is a 'breaker of cities' who never becomes a 'shepherd of the people'. His glorious life is short, as is that of 'the superb Hygelac', Beowulf's own lord, who falls in a freebooting raid on the Rhine. The heroic ideal of unflinching individual courage, of a glorious personal transcendence of human limitations, is married in *Beowulf* to the complementary ideals of responsibility towards kindred and of mutual service between a lord and his people. Thus, Hrothgar the Dane is a patriarch, an idealized lord like Charlemagne or Arthur, and he and his lady Wealhtheow dispense in Heorot the goods of peace. He is heir to an empire built up by the heroic aggression of the founder, Scyld, and he shares the goods of empire in Heorot. Like Bede's sparrow passing from darkness to darkness through the lighted hall in the twinkling of an eye, Scyld comes from the sea and returns to the sea. When the stability of the 'careless' life of Heorot is destroyed by the outsider Grendel, Hrothgar is saved by the service of another seaborne outsider, Beowulf, who, like Scyld, is a kind of orphan. Beowulf purges Heorot of Grendel and his mother; but the future of Denmark is dark. At Hrothgar's feet sits Unferth, who has killed his own kinsmen. Hrothgar's nephew and co-ruler, Hrothulf, brought up like a son, will after Hrothgar's death kill his son. Hrothgar is to marry his daughter, Freawaru, to Ingeld the Heathobard in what Beowulf foresees as a vain effort to heal the tribal feud, which in its last outbreak will lead to the burning down of Heorot and to the end of the Heathobards. At home in Geatland – to pursue this 'social' theme – Beowulf gives all his prizes to his lord Hygelac, with the thane-like words:

> 'I rejoice to present them. Joy, for me, always
> lies in your gift. Little family
> do I have in the world, Hygelac, besides yourself.' (2148–50)

After Hygelac's calamitous death, his nephew Beowulf serves his son Heardred, and assumes the kingdom only when there is no one else to do so (a contrast with Hrothulf). He protects his people for fifty years, and gives Wiglaf his dying voice. But Beowulf, son of an exile, has no son. He is irreplaceable. The gold he won for his people – the embodied glory of a race of men – is returned to the ground 'as useless to men as it was before'. No one shall inherit: the gold and the glory are buried with him. The cycle of the heroic life would then seem, in paradigm, to run as follows: young founders, builders and defenders (Scyld, Hrothgar, Beowulf) enjoy a time of prosperity, but in old age the 'troops of friends' cannot be relied on. The warlike are killed (Hygelac, Ongentheow), the peaceable eventually fall through accident (Hrethel) or frailty (Hrothgar).

The story shows the limits of heroism in the failure of the young companions and through the modification of the ideal hero from the adventurer Sigemund to the relatively *pius* Beowulf, who is *monna mildust*, 'the mildest of men', as well as *lof-geornost*, 'keenest for fame'. For a northern hero, Beowulf is ceremonious, eloquent, courteous, modest, almost urbane. It is only when taunted by the egregious Unferth that he boasts of his swimming-match with Breca. And he returns the sword that Unferth had lent him for the fight against Grendel's mother with gracious thanks, making no mention of the fact that in the fight it had failed. (Wiglaf is also gentlemanly: his report of the dragon-fight reduces the decisiveness of his own intervention.) Beowulf has a velvet glove as well as an iron hand. By northern standards, he is a very gentle bear: a hero who is also an ideal thane and lord. His death, though tragic, is glorious, like that of Bryhtnoth in *The Battle of Maldon*. When he was young his companions had tried to help him, but at home, in old age, he is deserted by them. He had wasted his armour on them, says Wiglaf. The days of heroism are over.

Another aspect of the poem shows the cost of the old law of vengeance. The sword is called *woruld-ræden*, 'the world's remedy', when it is placed on the lap of Hengest as a reminder of the duty of revenge. This comes shortly after the scene of the Danish princess Hildeburgh standing by the funeral pyre of her brother and her son:

> There were melting heads
> and bursting wounds, as the blood sprang out
> from weapon-bitten bodies. Blazing fire,
> most insatiable of spirits, swallowed the remains
> of the victims of both nations. Their valour was no more.
>
> (1119–23)

A few lines later Hildeburgh is to lose her husband, slain by Hengest. The Frisian episode is reported by Hrothgar's poet as a Danish 'away win', successfully avenging treachery as the code required. His song contrasts with the song of Creation at the opening of Heorot. What might Hildeburgh think of 'the world's remedy', the sword of vengeance?

Beowulf is a good hero and a good king, but is son of Edgetheow, who killed a man and set off the greatest of all feuds, according to Hrothgar. Names in the poem often compound two elements, and these compounds usually do not have meaning. Yet Edge ('Sword') + Theowa ('Servant') = Servant of the Sword, and in *Beowulf* the sword fails Edgetheow's son. He renounces its use against Grendel, a descendant of the first fratricide. It turns out that Grendel is invulnerable to swords. Against Grendel's mother, Beowulf uses Hrunting, a sword lent him by Unferth, who has used it against a kinsman. Hrunting does not hurt Grendel's mother. Providence then provides Beowulf with a giant-sword. On the hilt is engraved the story of the Flood in which God had drowned the Giants (although some monsters survive under water). Against the dragon, Beowulf's own sword fails; only after Wiglaf has pierced the dragon can Beowulf finish it off with a knife. Swords are no use to Beowulf, as the poet points out.

What are the monsters, and why do they attack? Grendel is a folklore troll converted by the poet into a descendant of Cain, who had killed his brother out of envy, and was marked and exiled by God. According to one explanation of the subsequent story, the children of Cain interbred with the children of Seth, the third child of Adam and Eve, producing giants and monsters, who were drowned in the Flood. Grendel is man, beast and demon, all three. He embodies envy and aggression, an uncivilized beast, whose name suggests cannibalism. He is also a demon: his eyes are full of hellish light, and his mother's blood melts the giant-sword. Yet he is also human, a human whose envy and blood-lust have made him a monster. His aggression is unprovoked, except by the sound of human enjoyment, whereas his mother has vengeance as a motive.

Treasure-guarding dragons come ultimately from classical legend. An Old English proverb says that old dragons live in mounds, guarding buried treasure. This may be connected with the curse upon grave-goods, so that arms buried for use in the next world should not be re-used by men. This dragon also flies by night, shooting forth flame. The *Anglo-Saxon Chronicle* entry for 793 records that dragons had been seen in the sky off Lindisfarne. The thunder-cloud is described in the third of the Riddles in the Exeter Book as a terrifying beast which shoots forth a bolt of fire which can kill a man.[10] Flying dragons are often found in Anglo-Saxon art, as for example on the Sutton Hoo helmet. In the *Chronicle* the dragons are an omen of the Viking attack upon Lindisfarne which followed soon after; the monastery was burned. The Viking longship often had a prow shaped as a dragon's head. Lightning too could set fire to the roofs of houses. Setting fire to the thatch was a good way to get defenders out of a house, used at the climax of *Njal's Saga*, and also in *Finnsburh*. (For a translation of this independent poetic fragment concerning the fight at Finnsburh recounted at *Beowulf* 1067ff., see p. 114.) The dragon in *Beowulf* responds to the theft of a cup from its hoard by burning down Beowulf's hall. Ethically the hoard-guarding dragon may symbolize possessive meanness, the opposite of the generosity of a ring-giver. The dragon might also more pointedly suggest the threat of a coastal raid from the hall-burning Vikings in their dragon-ships. The three monsters, on this reading, symbolize respectively unprovoked aggression, the law of vengeance and greed for gold. All three were characteristic of Vikings – and also, further back, of the conquering ancestors of Anglo-Saxon kings.

The poem may warn an Anglo-Saxon ruler against the complacency of Hrothgar. Beowulf's own funeral shows his destiny as obscure, like Scyld's, although a crucial earlier line seems to accord him salvation. In any case, it is clear that he is regarded positively as an ideal hero, a cleanser and protector, even if heroism is not enough, since even at its most defensive it accepts the law of vengeance. Human swords fail the hero. If, as the text is usually read to mean, Beowulf is mourned by a Geatish woman, this figure of the mourning woman must recall the sorrow of the Danish princess Hildeburgh, and also the misgivings which Wealhtheow feels about her sons, and the fears which Beowulf has for Hrothgar's daughter Freawaru, given in marriage-alliance to the son of an old enemy. It seems that part of the meaning of *Beowulf* is mediated through the figure of the mourning woman, the woman whose feelings are sacrificed to the law of vengeance. In this sense, the meaning of *Beowulf* is Hildeburgh:

> Sorrowful princess!
> This decree of fate the daughter of Hoc
> mourned with good reason; for when morning came
> the clearness of heaven disclosed to her
> the murder of those kindred who were the cause of all
> her earthly bliss.   (1074–9)

Theme and Development

If the characteristics of epic are inclusiveness of range, objectivity of treatment, unity of ethos and a significant action, then *Beowulf* is an epic of the same kind as the classical epics. Readers unimpressed by the title of epic may find in *Beowulf* a breadth and depth, a resonance and dignity that they might not expect to find in a glorified folk-tale full of interesting historical material, which is how the poem used to be presented. The life and death of the hero recapitulate the cycle of an age: the heroic generation is born, flourishes and dies. On to the elemental power of the original tale or myth the teller has grafted a set of human and social themes, so that the single-handed adventure comes to express the struggle of the forces of life and death in human society and human nature, and the monsters become malign embodiments of human evil. The struggle of the *aglæcas* ('terrible ones' – a name given to Beowulf as well as to the monsters) is part of a general struggle of the forces of harmony with the forces of destruction.

This conflict first manifests itself powerfully with the coming of Grendel, but there are auguries of his coming in the account of the founding of the Scylding dynasty. We learn that Scyld took away the mead-benches of terrified local tribes; that the 'lordless' Danes themselves had been unprotected before his coming; and immediately after the first feast in Heorot we have a veiled allusion to the burning down of 'the world's palace' in the last outbreak of the Heathobard feud. The serene hymn of the Cædmon-like poet to the creative achievement of Heorot, an indoor Eden, a *yeard* within the *middanyeard*, seems almost to provoke the irruption of Grendel into the poem.

> So the company of men led a careless life,
> all was well with them: until One began
> to encompass evil, an enemy from hell.   (98–100)

The warmth and light which went into the description of Heorot
now reappear reversed in the description of Grendel. Reversal and
dualism characterize the structure and the dynamics of the poem.
But even before Grendel appears we have become acquainted with
evil and pain in Scyld's ripped-out mead-benches, the desolation
of the lordless Danes, Scyld's death and the treacherous burning
down of Heorot; good and evil are intertwined from the beginning,
and Grendel appears as the emanation of all those envious forces
which are driven to destroy the music and laughter of Heorot.
The poem works off opposition: the attraction and repulsion
between the positive and negative poles can be felt in its every
part – not only between God and the demons, the hero and the
monsters, the true and the false thane, but in all its values,
movement and imagery. The social images of the poem are like
those in *Macbeth*: light, feasting, order and ceremony on the one
hand, darkness, murder, disorder and savagery on the other – 'You
have displaced the mirth, broke the good meeting/With most
admired disorder.' The public celebration of social unity is the
sharing out at the feast of food, drink, gold and, above all, of
words: its antithesis is Grendel's grinding and swallowing of his
enemies, uncooked, in silent, solitary, nocturnal, cannibalistic joy
– and this in the hall of the feast! The after-dinner conversation
of the birds and beasts of carrion on the battlefield is another
repulsive anti-type of the feast of life. Such violent oppositions,
contrasts and comparisons can be found at every stage of the
poem.

The wrestling of Beowulf and Grendel is powerfully suggestive:

> Fear entered into
> the listening North Danes, as that noise rose up again
> strange and strident. It shrilled terror
> to the ears that heard it through the hall's side-wall,
> the grisly plaint of God's enemy,
> his song of ill-success, the sobs of the damned one
> bewailing his pain. (782–8)

Grendel had felt hatred and rage at hearing the song of Creation through the same walls. Sometimes the paired comparisons can seem schematic, as in the elaborate exclamations over the double death of hero and dragon. But this elaboration and orchestration of the primitive conflict of Beowulf and Grendel into an epic conflict between life and death, harmony and chaos, good and evil, is unmistakable. The thematic development is conscious: the tracing of Grendel's envy and hatred back to Cain's fratricide and the Giants' rebellion involves a theory of evil. The *morthor-hete*, the murderous hatred of individuals and of tribes, takes on the pattern of a blood-feud within the family of the children of men. The duty to avenge a slain kinsman is absolute. Property and territorial rights are also sacred: great stress is laid on the ownership of land, halls, cups and armour. The stolen drinking-cup belongs to the last survivor of the race who buried it, and to the dragon, its guardian. Even Grendel may receive pity as a disinherited exile, an outcast from life's feast by inheritance of blood. These laws of motive and necessary effect bind the action. Beowulf himself provokes no unnecessary fights and swears no unrightful oaths; but he feels obliged to help the exiled Eadgils to his vengeance. The poem opposes treacherous fratricide to firm friendship. This focus on the tragic consequences of the unappeasable feud in *Beowulf* is Germanic, but Cain's question at Genesis 4:9 can be heard: 'Am I my brother's keeper?'

Another motif of the poem, the destruction of whole societies, symbolized by the empty and silent hall, is traditional in Old English poetry. Elegies such as *The Wanderer* are affected by Christian ideas of the transitoriness of this world and its imminent end; if *The Ruin* laments glories now past, *The Wanderer* finally points to the heavenly remedy. (The same grief is felt in the Welsh *Gododdin* of *c*.600, and in the lament for Cynddylan's hall.[11]) The *Beowulf*-poet constantly connects the nightmare of the empty hall with the destructiveness of the blood-feud, and in his critique of heroic society the Christian element shows in the ideal of a more God-fearing, responsible and civilized hero. There is also a Christian element in the comments on the dragon's gold. But Beowulf's desire to fight the dragon alone, though its outcome is tragic, is admirable in a defender of his people. The emphasis is not upon individual morality but upon *wyrd*, the inevitable pattern of things. Those who see *Beowulf* as a reformist Christian poem sometimes allegorize the dragon as the dragon of the Apocalypse or Beowulf as a type of the Christian saviour. In Denmark, the poet reproves Danish idol-worship, and gives Grendel a biblical ancestry. He often remarks on God's mastery of human affairs, and has Hrothgar deliver a homily to Beowulf about pride. But this Christian perspective is much less evident after Beowulf returns to Geatland.

Other differences between the Danish and Geatish halves of the poem raise a question about the genesis of *Beowulf*. The transition of Anglo-Saxon verse from oral composition to writing is obscure. The original, an unknown number of stages behind our manuscript, may not have been the work of a single literary author. The poem falls into uneven halves, the second, beginning at line 2199, different in structure and content. Its history is less social, more warlike. Its monster is less folkloric, more fictional and symbolic. It has no picture of life at Beowulf's court, and more reminiscence and prophecy than present narrative. There are many 'sad stories of the death of kings'. Hrethel's death and the last survivor's lament generalize a concern with mortality. *Beowulf* as a whole has clear unity of theme, even if its narrative parts were once separate. Also, Beowulf's repetitions to Hrothgar of the fight at the Mere and to Hygelac of the whole Danish adventure vary interestingly from the poet's first account – an 'oral' inconsistency.

This Introduction has considered *Beowulf* in the perspective of comparative literature, as an epic, and stressed the debts its form and technique owe to traditions of oral composition. This is not to imply that *Beowulf* is as great as the *Iliad* or *Odyssey*, still less that it is heathen. Since the majority of texts surviving from the eighth century and after are the works of Latin Christianity, *Beowulf* has increasingly been studied in that context. Literary rhetoric and oral composition have in common many techniques designed to aid extempore improvisation and declamation – they both use procedures of amplification and variation upon a typical theme. If 'the *Beowulf*-poet' is anything like what he is supposed to be, he had heard and read sermons and saints' lives, and had learned from their techniques – as did Cædmon, whom Bede presents as our first Christian poet. But, like the illiterate Cædmon, 'the *Beowulf*-poet' could never have begun to compose verse unless he had already mastered a vernacular tradition, originally oral and very different in style from rhymed Latin hymns or Silver Latin elegiacs. It was this Germanic tradition of oral composition that supplied him with his versification and his repertoire of themes and narrative devices and verbal formulae. It may have supplied him with a *Beowulf*-kit, and perhaps an oral *Beowulf*. It is now a written poem, not an oral one. But a written oral poem, like a film of a play, makes more sense when the conventions of the former medium are recognized.

Narration

An introduction to a translation is not the place to show the impress of oral-formulaic composition on the detail of the original. But the narration of *Beowulf* also shows signs of oral tradition: it has type-scenes which are themselves narrative formulae – the banquet, the battle, the boast, the voyage, the funeral – and which arrange themselves into envelope and interlace patterns.

As the poem unfolds, its thematic coherence emerges. It is clear that the purpose of the parallels to the main story is one of ethical comparison, even if this legendary history is not always clear. The historical episodes are sometimes allusive, and in allusion there is a certain riddling delight in making the point at issue not too obvious. At our cultural distance, notes are needed, and in this second edition of the translation, the notes have been much amplified.

To those who expect physical action, *Beowulf* may seem something of an oratorio. The Grendel-fight is powerful, but not very detailed. The Hygelac–Ongentheow episode has more conventionally exciting warfare. *Beowulf* can be slow, lacking in suspense, full of speeches and authorial asides. It is aural rather than visual. It is as much a meditation upon an action as an action. And, even more than most works, it only makes full sense if considered not only as a single series of events in time but also as a completed pattern of events. *Beowulf* is full of anticipations, comparisons and flashbacks. Heorot is an example we have looked at: we are told that it is to be burned almost before it is built. Likewise Scyld's funeral gets more prominence than his life. This temporal foreshortening, so that everything is narrated in the light of its known outcome, is characteristic of ballads: we are told the results of the first and last monster-fights in advance and reminded of the outcome of all three more than once. Beowulf's fifty-year reign takes up one line, and we are then told how the dragon's hoard is robbed before we know how either gold or dragon got there. Geatish history is likewise recounted in an order more thematic than chronological.

Style

The tales being traditional, the interest of the audience was all in the telling and in comparison with parallel events. They liked artful elaboration and fullness in banquets and speeches and armour; but action is presented less by visual particulars than by means of its material effects – often sound effects. There is a consistent metonymy: we hear the footsteps of Beowulf, the scream of Grendel, the horn of Hygelac, the jingle of a mail-shirt. Indirectness and metaphor are endemic in the poetic style. The sun is 'the sky's candle' or 'heaven's jewel'; Beowulf is 'Hygelac's thane' or 'Hrothgar's monster-warden'; the dragon is 'the barrow's guardian' or 'night's alone-flier'; God is 'glory's wielder' or 'victory's bestower'. This habit of providing alternative names in the form of a genitive relation between two other nouns, often images, is conventionally praised for its vividness ('swan's riding' or 'whale's acre' as kennings for the sea), but the vividness is often intellectual rather than visual, imagistic or concrete. To refer to battle as 'the sword-play' is characteristic: it abstracts and schematizes, it disguises and elevates. The painful confusion of battle is, by an ironic euphemism, transformed into a game of objects, beautiful and bloodless. This euphemistic stress on effects can, by leaving so much to the imagination, intensify the reality of what is being described – or half-described. Wiglaf's speech over Beowulf's body has all these characteristics:

> 'Now the flames shall grow dark
> and the fire destroy the sustainer of the warriors
> who often endured the iron shower
> when, string-driven, the storm of arrows
> sang over shield-wall, and the shaft did its work,
> sped by its feathers, furthered the arrow-head.' (3111–16)

The audience enjoyed the elaborate unstraightforwardness with which the expected is disguised. Laconic understatement and the use of the negative accomplish the same purpose. Wiglaf reports that 'little courtesy was shown in allowing me to pass/beneath the earth-wall' (3086–7): he had to kill the dragon to get inside the mound. This grim humour, to be found in Yorkshire and other parts settled by Scandinavians, comes in a more weighty and elaborate form in this comment on the dragon's first blitz upon the Geats:

> That was a fearful beginning
> for the people of that country; uncomfortable and swift
> was the end to be likewise for their lord and treasure-giver.
>
> (2308–10)

'As the beginning was to the people so the end would be to their lord': parallelism, antithesis and variation are the characteristics of the verbal style of *Beowulf* – which is considerably more embellished and involved than that of other Old English poetry. The syntax is correspondingly more sustained; but the 'lack of steady advance' Klaeber noted in the narrative is even more marked in the sentence. Traditional near-synonyms are juggled in dense apposition, so that the 'advance', always slow, is almost suspended. Thus:

Then Beowulf spoke; bent by smith's skill
the meshed rings of his mail-shirt glittered . . .
                              'To you I will now
put one request, Royal Scylding,
Shield of the South Danes, one sole favour
that you'll not deny me, dear lord of your people,
now that I have come thus far, Fastness of Warriors;
that I alone may be allowed, with my loyal and determined
crew of companions, to cleanse your hall Heorot.'

(405–6, 426–32)

The variation and parallelism of the poetic style distinguish it
from that of Homer. A test for 'orality' is that there should be no
duplication of formulae; that for any given essential idea, in any
given metrical position and grammatical form, there should be one
formula only. Though several formulae recur ('Beowulf spoke',
'protector of the people', 'heroes under heaven', 'grim and greedy',
'giver of rings', 'hard under helmet'), profusion rather than economy is the rule for synonyms and epithets. This may be because
Old English metre allows more variation than the Greek dactylic
hexameter, or because of the influence of literary rhetoric, or of
something in the Anglo-Saxon temperament. The effect is much
less simple, rapid and direct than Homer. There are simple half-
lines: 'He was a good king'; 'he chose his deathbed'; 'the journey
was over' – but they contrast with an antecedent amplitude. Thus,
of the dragon:

He had poured out fire and flame on the people,
he had put them to the torch; he trusted now to the barrow's
        walls
and to his fighting strength; his faith misled him.   (2320–22)

Many an eloquent verse-paragraph concludes with a pithy, often ironic, comment of this sort, and the contrast of elaboration and plainness, of raising up and knocking down, is marked. The way the sentences twist and twine back on themselves is like the wrestling beasts of Anglo-Saxon art: the eye is teased and bewildered by the fantastic convolutions of these abstract ribbon-like creatures that suddenly end in a small jewelled head and reveal themselves, not as a maze or a Celtic version of a Greek key, but as serpents. The denseness and allusiveness of *Beowulf*'s style are chiefly created by diction. The nouns and adjectives which make up most of the epic formulae are highly poetical – not only imaginative and beautiful but far-fetched and peculiar to poetry; they often contain a fossilized animistic metaphor. The vocabulary (and word order) of Old English prose is simpler and more analytic. The traditional and stylized quality of the poetic diction is difficult to convey in translation without recourse to archaism. The Old English diction is special and archaic but not archaizing, and strenuous rather than mellifluous.

Verse

This power of diction is a response of language to metrical constraint. The key to Old English metre is the pause in the middle of the line: the two halves of the line on either side of the break are felt to be equal in weight, each half-line normally consisting of a phrase with two stressed and two or more unstressed syllables. (The basis of the metre is stress or accent, not the quantity nor the number of the syllables.) A typical line might be:

the fell and fen   his fastness was.

A line therefore consists of two units ultimately identical in their general metrical form. The essence of the metre is the theoretical norm: 'two is to two as two is to two', where the 'twos' represent two syllables, one stressed, the other not. Actual lines vary this symmetry. The Old English metre is often called 'the alliterative measure', a term best kept for the verse of the alliterative revival of later medieval centuries, which has lost the economy of Old English. The alliteration, though compulsory and distinctive, is less fundamental than the stress pattern which it signals.[12]

The rule is that the first sound in the first stressed syllable in the second half-line must also begin one of the two stressed syllables in the first half-line. The other stressed syllable in the first half-line may alliterate; the last stressed syllable in the line normally should not. Thus, of the four stresses in the line, the first and/or the second must alliterate with the third, and the fourth be different. Only the four fully stressed syllables of the line enter into this calculation, and it is necessary to distinguish a fully stressed from a half-stressed syllable. All vowels alliterate. This account ignores the refinements of the system which deal with extra and missing syllables and stresses. The alliteration binds the half-lines together over the break and emphasizes this symmetry. The stressed syllables are also the most important syllables from the point of view of the sense. Nouns and adjectives rank above verbs, and there is a grammatical and syntactic hierarchy in the kinds of half-lines permitted to begin sentences. The sentences are built up of formulaic phrases, each half a line long, and the sense, as Milton prescribed for 'true musical delight', is 'variously drawn out from one verse into another'. Traditional oral composition by phrase accounts for an exclamatory lack of syntactic subordination, and for the tacking, resumptive movement of the sense: two steps forward, one step back.

Today, 'Anglo-Saxon' is a term popularly used for words which are blunt and physical. Anglo-Saxon verse was not like that. The pleasure of it is of variety in unity, freedom within form: it arises from the play between the demands of the sense and those of the metre. The symmetry of the halves of the line produces balance, antithesis and chiasmus much more commonly than in unrhymed iambic pentameter, and the forward movement is much more impeded than in later English blank verse. The halves of the line are often not in the natural sequence of prose or spoken syntax, and, as the mind reshuffles the parts of the sentence, the half-lines may move apart; but alliteration and the stress pattern bind them together. The final impression of the verse in *Beowulf*, then, is of contrasting energies held in a rhythmic balance.

I conclude with words from the poem's most distinguished recent editor, my late colleague George Jack: 'In his command of metrical form and the resources of style the *Beowulf*-poet shows exceptional gifts. His metrical usage conforms to extremely precise constraints, and his style is distinguished particularly by its richness in the use of compound words and by its control of syntactic form. In these respects, as in the power and range of its narrative, *Beowulf* is a work of outstanding accomplishment.'[13]

Translating Beowulf

This translation began with the desire to catch in modern English some of the mastery of the Old English verse of the original. As the attempt to imitate the art of its verse and syntax was prolonged, the deeper pattern and the substance and significance of the poem began to emerge. Some translators of *Beowulf*, like William Morris, Edwin Morgan, Kevin Crossley-Holland and Seamus Heaney, have not been Anglo-Saxon scholars. Undeterred by its difficulty, they were perhaps attracted less by the subject-matter than by the style. That is certainly the case with myself.

Beowulf can stand on its own without introduction by a transla-tor. But since this version first appeared in 1973, I have found that poetic translation itself is not generally understood. Scholarly reviewers concentrated on the Introduction and avoided the trans-lation, perhaps because they did not wish to speak evil but also perhaps because they were not sure how to evaluate a translation which had aims beyond those of accuracy, the criterion by which modern scholarly translation is usually judged. Accuracy is easier in prose. Unliterary folk have asked why I translated something that has been translated before. Students are surprised to discover that translations differ. Scholars have asked me why I translate a particular word in a particular way, or even why the same word is not always translated in the same way. Translations which would satisfy such tests would not satisfy those who look at a translation to see why the original is supposed to be of interest.

One of the aims of this translation was to observe, as far as I could without putting undue strain on idiom, the rules governing Old English metre, so as to recreate its different rhythm. This was hard, because modern English has fewer inflections, and more small relational words, than Old English. It was difficult to keep to the alliterative rules, and to keep the economy of words and syllables. I have estimated that each line of the translation took about one hour. Lines and sentences had to be recast again and again. At worst it was like knitting a crossword. Two other aims I had were to keep as close to the sense as I could, and to attempt to match the style. Aiming to reproduce metre, sense and style means juggling three aims. A translation cannot reproduce even one of these three things completely, for languages, and the cultures they articulate, can be very different. The difficulties of keeping the metre have been mentioned. Determining sense can also be

difficult, and the finding of an acceptable rendering involves sacrifices. Finally, the creation of a suitably appropriate equivalent
style in modern English depends on the view of the poem as a
whole. My first translations for *The Earliest English Poems*, done in
the early 1960s, did not avoid archaism. As I translated the poems
for that selection, I gradually renounced archaism, although I
continued to take risks with diction; a short poem can afford to be
more daring. But an epic has as its norm a steadier style. *Beowulf*,
compared with the shorter poems, is more reserved and dignified
and has a more wrought style and syntax. It has a high incidence
of archaic poetic locutions.[14]

In a translation such as I intended, the blend of metre, syntax,
diction and idiom in the artistic economy of the original can only
be done by redistributing the rarer effects. Each line and sentence
necessarily sacrifices some quality in the original. What you lose
here, you hope to restore there. A translation built as a whole
should not be assessed brick by verbal brick. One example must
suffice: the line and a half giving the scene in Heorot on the
morning after Grendel's attack, *Þær wæs æfter wiste   wop up
ahafen,/micel morgensweg*. This means literally: 'After the feasting
an outburst of weeping was raised up, much noise in the morning'
(127–8). This is rendered:

> night's table-laughter turned to morning's
> lamentation.

The juxtaposition of *wiste* and *wop* (feasting and weeping) cannot
be directly reproduced, but I tried for an analogous effect with a
quiet play on 'mourning' and on turning the tables. Such riddling
word-play is not uncommon in the original. I was not dissatisfied
with this, but elsewhere I sometimes had to settle for more serious
shortcomings. Scholars who find the version too free have to

consider whether literal prose does not too freely discard the potential advantages of verse. I used to think that all prose translation of poetry of this sort was useless. That was before I read a number of verse translations. Prose translation can be useful, and more than useful – the English of Garmonsway's version has dignity and rhythmical shape. Most prose translations, however, are drab, and make it a virtue to fall so short that the translation cannot be confused with the real thing. A poetic translation is an attempt to offer an equivalent poem to those who cannot read the original. It is an equivalent, not a substitute. This was the aim of the best translators in English: Chaucer, Marlowe, Jonson, Dryden, Pope. The Old English poets are represented as composing to a stringed instrument, so the performance had a musical aspect. I do not expect readers to chant, but I hope they will read the verse aloud. *Beowulf* was not written to be readable but to be listened to.

Notes

1. The closing lines of the poem on the battle of Brunanburh, trans. Michael Alexander, *The Earliest English Poems*, 3rd edn (Penguin Books, Harmondsworth, 1991).

2. This opinion is based on the linguistic and metrical tests applied by Fulk and accepted by George Jack in his Introduction to *Beowulf: A Student Edition* (Clarendon Press, Oxford, 1994), p. xx. The dating of the poem is well discussed in 'Date, Provenance, Authors, Audiences', chapter 2 of *A Beowulf Handbook*, ed. Robert E. Bjork and John D. Niles (University of Nebraska Press, Lincoln, Nebraska, 1997).

3. For Bede, see D. H. Farmer (ed.), *Bede's Ecclesiastical History of the English People* etc., trans. Leo Sherley-Price, rev. edn (Penguin Books, Harmondsworth, 1990). Cædmon's *Hymn* is translated in Michael Alexander, *Earliest English Poems*. For accounts of Old English poetry, see

Michael Alexander's *History of Old English Literature*, 3rd edn (Broadview, Peterborough, Ontario, 2001), and *The Cambridge Companion to Old English Literature*, ed. Michael Lapidge and Malcolm Godden (Cambridge University Press, Cambridge, 1991).

4. Michael Alexander, 'Tennyson's *Battle of Brunanburh*', *Tennyson Research Bulletin*, vol. 4, no. 4 (Nov. 1985), 151–61.

5. See the chapter 'Translations, Versions, Illustrations' by Marijane Osborne in Robert E. Bjork and John D. Niles, *Handbook*.

6. Hesiod, *Works and Days* 156–66, trans. Dorothea Wender (Penguin Books, Harmondsworth, 1972).

7. See J. R. R. Tolkien, '*Beowulf*: the Monsters and the Critics', *Proceedings of the British Academy*, 22 (1936), 245–95, 1937, on the poem's relation to Norse mythology. Also the chapter by Roberta Frank in Michael Lapidge and Malcolm Godden (eds.), *Cambridge Companion*.

8. Northrop Frye, *Anatomy of Criticism* (Princeton University Press, Princeton, NJ, 1957), 105.

9. For a translation of *The Dream of the Rood*, see Michael Alexander, *Earliest English Poems*.

10. See Michael Alexander, *Old English Riddles from the Exeter Book*, 2nd edn (Anvil Press Poetry, London, 1984).

11. Translated in J. P. Clancy, *The Earliest Welsh Poetry* (Macmillan, London, 1970).

12. For a clear account of the verse, see D. G. Scragg, 'The Nature of Old English Verse', in Michael Lapidge and Malcolm Godden (eds), *Cambridge Companion*.

13. Cited from George Jack's entry on *Beowulf* in *The Blackwell Encyclopaedia of Anglo-Saxon England*, ed. Michael Lapidge, John Blair, Simon Keynes, Donald Scragg (Blackwell, Oxford and Malden, Mass., 1999).

14. 'Old English Poetry into Modern English Verse', *Translation and Literature*, vol. 3 (Edinburgh University Press, Edinburgh, 1994), 69–75.

Genealogical Tables

1. The royal house of the Danes (Scyldings)

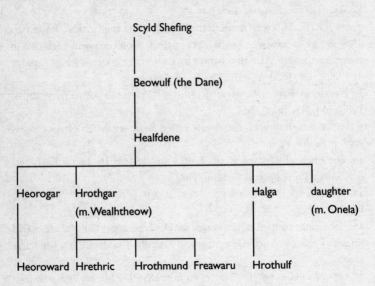

2. *The royal house of the Geats*

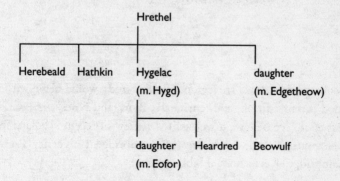

Hrethel

Herebeald   Hathkin   Hygelac   daughter
                        (m. Hygd)   (m. Edgetheow)

daughter   Heardred   Beowulf
(m. Eofor)

3. *The royal house of the Swedes (Scylfings)*

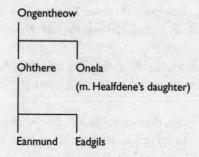

Ongentheow

Ohthere   Onela
           (m. Healfdene's daughter)

Eanmund   Eadgils

Further Reading

Books about *Beowulf* are legion. Further study would begin with a good recent edition, and, currently, Bjork and Niles's *A Beowulf Handbook* (see below), a well-edited review of recent scholarship. The journal *Anglo-Saxon England* (Cambridge University Press, Cambridge) has an annual bibliography.

Editions

Alexander, Michael, *Beowulf: A Glossed Text*, Penguin English Poets (Penguin Books, Harmondsworth and New York, 1995; revised edn, 2000)

Davis, N., *Beowulf*, a facsimile with facing transcription. The Early English Text Society (Oxford University Press, London, 1966)

Dobbie, E. V. K. (ed.), *Beowulf and Judith*. The Anglo-Saxon Poetic Records IV (Columbia University Press, New York, 1953)

Jack, George (ed.), *Beowulf: A Student Edition* (Clarendon Press, Oxford, 1994)

Kiernan, Kevin S. (ed.), *Electronic Beowulf on CD-ROM* (British Library, London, 2000)

Klaeber, F., *Beowulf and the Fight at Finnsburg*, ed. with Introduction, Bibliography, Notes, Glossary and Appendices, 3rd edn with two supplements (D. C. Heath, Boston; Harrap, London, 1950)

Mitchell, B., and Robinson, F. C., (eds.), *Beowulf: An Edition* (Blackwell, Oxford, 1998)

Swanton, Michael (ed.), *Beowulf* (Manchester University Press, Manchester, 1978)

Wrenn, C. L. (ed.), *Beowulf*, 5th edn, revised by W. F. Bolton (Exeter University Press, Exeter, 1996)

Language

Davis, N., *Sweet's Anglo-Saxon Primer* (Clarendon Press, Oxford, 1953)

Mitchell, B., and Robinson, F. C., *A Guide to Old English*, 5th edn (Blackwell, Oxford, and Cambridge, Mass., 1994)

Quirk, R., and Wrenn, C. L., *An Old English Grammar*, 2nd edn (Methuen, London, 1963)

Translations

Clark Hall, J., and Wrenn, C. L., *Beowulf and the Finnesburg Fragment*, a Translation into Modern English Prose, with Prefatory Remarks by J. R. R. Tolkien, 2nd edn (Allen & Unwin, London, 1950)

Garmonsway, G. N., and Simpson, J., *Beowulf and its Analogues* (Dent and Dutton, London and New York, 1968)

Heaney, Seamus, *Beowulf: A New Translation* (Faber, London, 1999)

Studies

Bjork, Robert E., and Niles, John D., *A Beowulf Handbook* (University of Nebraska Press, Lincoln, Nebraska, 1997)

Bonjour, A., *The Digressions in Beowulf* (Blackwell, Oxford, 1950)

Bradley, S. A. (ed. and trans.), *Anglo-Saxon Poetry* (Dent, London, 1982; Charles E. Tuttle, Boston, Mass., 1991)

Brodeur, A. G., *The Art of Beowulf* (University of California Press, Berkeley and Los Angeles, 1959)

Chambers, R. W., *Beowulf, an Introduction*, 3rd edn, with a supplement by C. L. Wrenn (Cambridge University Press, Cambridge, 1959). See also '*Beowulf* and the Heroic Age in England' in R. W. Chambers, *Man's Unconquerable Mind* (Cape, London, 1939)

Chase, C. (ed.), *The Dating of Beowulf* (University of Toronto Press, Toronto, 1981)

Clark, G., *Beowulf* (Twayne, Boston, 1990)

Irving, E. B., Jr, *A Reading of Beowulf* (Yale University Press, New Haven, 1968)

— *Rereading Beowulf* (Pennsylvania University Press, Philadelphia, 1989)

Nicholson, L. E. (ed.), *An Anthology of Beowulf Criticism* (University of Notre Dame Press, Notre Dame, 1963)

Niles, J. D., *Beowulf: The Poem and its Tradition* (Harvard University Press, Cambridge, Mass., 1983)

Robinson, F. C., *Beowulf and the Appositive Style* (University of Tennessee Press, Knoxville, 1985)

— *The Tomb of Beowulf and Other Essays on Old English* (Blackwell, Oxford, 1993)

Shippey, T. A., *Beowulf* (Edward Arnold, London, 1978; Charles River Books, Boston, Mass., 1979)

Sisam, K., *The Structure of Beowulf* (Clarendon Press, Oxford, 1965)

Tolkien, J. R. R., '*Beowulf*: the Monsters and the Critics', *Proceedings of the British Academy*, 22 (1936), 245–95, 1937; included in L. E. Nicholson, *Anthology*

Whitelock, D., *The Audience of Beowulf*, 2nd edn (Clarendon Press, Oxford, 1958)

Contexts

Alexander, Michael (ed. and trans.), *Old English Riddles from the Exeter Book*, 2nd edn (Anvil Press Poetry, London, 1984)

— *A History of Old English Literature*, 3rd edn (Broadview, Peterborough, Ontario, 2001)

— (ed. and trans.), *The Earliest English Poems*, 3rd edn (Penguin Books, Harmondsworth, 1991)

Blair, P. Hunter, *Introduction to Anglo-Saxon England* (Cambridge University Press, Cambridge, 1956)

— *The World of Bede* (*Studies in Anglo-Saxon England*) (Cambridge University Press, New York, 1990)

Bruce-Mitford, R. L. S. *et al.*, *The Sutton Hoo Ship Burial* (British Museum, London, 1975–83; W. Sessions (UK)/State Mutual Book and Periodical Service, New York, 1988)

Campbell, James (ed.), *The Anglo-Saxons* (Phaidon, Oxford, 1982; Viking Penguin, Harmondsworth and New York, 1991)

Chadwick, H. M., and Chadwick, N. K., *The Growth of Literature*, 3 vols (Cambridge University Press, Cambridge, 1932; New York, 1986)

Farmer, D. H. (ed.), *Bede's Ecclesiastical History of the English People* etc., trans. L. Sherley-Price, rev. edn (Penguin Books, Harmondsworth, 1990)

Fox, Denton, and Palsson, Hermann (trans.), *Grettir's Saga* (University of Toronto Press, Toronto, 1974; repr. 1981)

Fry, D. K. (ed.), *Finnsburh: Fragment and Episode* (Methuen, London, 1974)

Frye, Northrop, *The Anatomy of Criticism* (Princeton University Press, Princeton, NJ, 1957)

Ker, W. P., *Epic and Romance* (Macmillan, London, 1908)

—*The Dark Ages* (Blackwood, Edinburgh, 1904)

Lapidge, Michael, and Godden, Malcolm (eds.), *The Cambridge Companion to Old English Literature* (Cambridge University Press, Cambridge, 1991)

Lapidge, M., Blair, J., Keynes, S., Scragg, D. (eds.) *The Blackwell Encyclopaedia of Anglo-Saxon England* (Blackwell, Oxford and Malden, Mass., 1999)

Lord, A. B., *The Singer of Tales* (Harvard University Press, Cambridge, Mass., 1964)

Mitchell, Bruce, *An Invitation to Anglo-Saxon England* (Blackwell, Oxford, 1995)

A Note on the Text

The manuscript containing *Beowulf*, written about the year 1010, is in the British Library, where it is known as Cotton Vitellius A.xv., having once been shelved under a bust of the Emperor Vitellius in Sir Robert Cotton's library. There was a fire at this library in 1731, charring the edges of some leaves, which lost letters and words, a process that continued after the manuscript was transcribed in 1786–7. Modern editions print the Old English text with readings restored from these transcripts, and also with many emendations in places where the text has seemed defective. The modern editions are in substantial agreement, but differ in detail. The text used as a base for this translation can be found in *Beowulf: A Glossed Text*, ed. Michael Alexander, Penguin English Poets, published in 1995. This second edition of the *Verse Translation* brings it into line with the *Glossed Text* as revised in 2000.

Line-Numbering

Please note that the line numbers every ten lines refer to the text of this translation, not to the line-numbering of the original text in modern editions. Line-references in the Introduction and Notes also refer to this translation, not to the original. Quite often a new paragraph begins at the second half-line of a verse, which by modern printing convention is dropped to a new line of type. In such cases two lines of type count as a single line of verse. The original has 3,182 lines, some of which are incomplete because of damage to the manuscript; the translation has 3,179 lines. Names of major characters are printed in italic type on their first appearance.

BEOWULF

Attend!
>We have heard of the thriving of the throne of Denmark,
>how the folk-kings flourished in former days,
>how those royal athelings earned that glory.

>Was it not *Scyld Shefing* that shook the halls,
>took mead-benches, taught encroaching
>foes to fear him – who, found in childhood,
>lacked clothing? Yet he lived and prospered,
>grew in strength and stature under the heavens
>until the clans settled in the sea-coasts neighbouring
10 >over the whale-road all must obey him
>and give tribute. He was a good king!

>A boy child was afterwards born to Scyld,
>a young child in hall-yard, a hope for the people,
>sent them by God; the griefs long endured
>were not unknown to Him, the harshness of years
>without a lord. Therefore the life-bestowing
>Wielder of Glory granted them this blessing.
>Through the northern lands the name of Beow,
>the son of Scyld, sprang widely.
20 >For in youth an atheling should so use his virtue,
>give with a free hand while in his father's house,
>that in old age, when enemies gather,

established friends shall stand by him
and serve him gladly. It is by glorious action
that a man comes by honour in any people.

At the hour shaped for him Scyld departed,
the hero crossed into the keeping of his Lord.
They carried him out to the edge of the sea,
his sworn arms-fellows, as he had himself desired them
30   while he wielded his words, Warden of the Scyldings,
beloved folk-founder; long had he ruled.

A boat with a ringed neck rode in the haven,
icy, out-eager, the atheling's vessel,
and there they laid out their lord and master,
dealer of wound gold, in the waist of the ship,
in majesty by the mast. A mound of treasures
from far countries was fetched aboard her,
and it is said that no boat was ever more bravely fitted
        out
with the weapons of a warrior, war accoutrement,
40   swords and body-armour; on his breast were set
treasures and trappings to travel with him
on his far faring into the flood's sway.

This hoard was not less great than the gifts he had had
from those who at the outset had adventured him
over seas, alone, a small child.

High over head they hoisted and fixed
a gold *signum*; gave him to the flood,
let the seas take him, with sour hearts
and mourning mood. Men under heaven's

50   shifting skies, though skilled in counsel,
      cannot say surely who unshipped that cargo.

      Then for a long space there lodged in the stronghold
      Beowulf the Dane, dear king of his people,
      famed among nations – his father had taken
      leave of the land – when late was born to him
      the lord Healfdene, lifelong the ruler
      and war-feared patriarch of the proud Scyldings.
      He next fathered four children
      that leapt into the world, this leader of armies,
60   Heorogar and *Hrothgar* and Halga the Good;
      and Ursula, I have heard, who was Onela's queen,
      knew the bed's embrace of the Battle-Scylfing.

      Then to Hrothgar was granted glory in battle,
      mastery of the field; so friends and kinsmen
      gladly obeyed him, and his band increased
      to a great company. It came into his mind
      that he would command the construction
      of a huge mead-hall, a house greater
      than men on earth ever had heard of,
70   and share the gifts God had bestowed on him
      upon its floor with folk young and old –
      apart from public land and the persons of slaves.
      Far and wide (as I heard) the work was given out
      in many a tribe over middle earth,
      the making of the mead-hall. And, as men reckon,
      the day of readiness dawned very soon
      for this greatest of houses. *Heorot* he named it
      whose word ruled a wide empire.
      He made good his boast, gave out rings,

80   arm-bands at the banquet. Boldly the hall reared
its arched gables; unkindled the torch-flame
that turned it to ashes. The time was not yet
when the blood-feud should bring out again
sword-hatred in sworn kindred.

It was with pain that the powerful spirit
dwelling in darkness endured that time,
hearing daily the hall filled
with loud amusement; there was the music of the harp,
the clear song of the poet, perfect in his telling
90   of the remote first making of man's race.
He told how, long ago, the Lord formed Earth,
a plain bright to look on, locked in ocean,
exulting established the sun and the moon
as lights to illumine the land-dwellers
and furnished forth the face of Earth
with limbs and leaves. Life He then granted
to each kind of creature that creeps and moves.

So the company of men led a careless life,
all was well with them: until One began
100   to encompass evil, an enemy from hell.
Grendel they called this cruel spirit,
the fell and fen his fastness was,
the march his haunt. This unhappy being
had long lived in the land of monsters
since the Creator cast them out
as kindred of *Cain*. For that killing of Abel
the eternal Lord took vengeance.
There was no joy of that feud: far from mankind
God drove him out for his deed of shame!

110 From Cain came down all kinds misbegotten
— ogres and elves and evil shades —
as also the Giants, who joined in long
wars with God. He gave them their reward.

With the coming of night came Grendel also,
sought the great house and how the Ring-Danes
held their hall when the horn had gone round.
He found in Heorot the force of nobles
slept after supper, sorrow forgotten,
the condition of men. Maddening with rage,
120 he struck quickly, creature of evil:
grim and greedy, he grasped on their pallets
thirty warriors, and away he was out of there,
thrilled with his catch: he carried off homeward
his glut of slaughter, sought his own halls.
As the day broke, with the dawn's light
Grendel's outrage was openly to be seen:
night's table-laughter turned to morning's
lamentation. Lord Hrothgar
sat silent then, the strong man mourned,
130 glorious king, he grieved for his thanes
as they read the traces of a terrible foe,
a cursed fiend. That was too cruel a feud,
too long, too hard!
                                   Nor did he let them rest
but the next night brought new horrors,
did more murder, manslaughter and outrage
and shrank not from it: he was too set on these things.

It was not remarked then if a man looked
for sleeping-quarters quieter, less central,

among the outer buildings; now openly shown,
140   the new hall-thane's hatred was manifest
and unmistakable. Each survivor
then kept himself at safer distance.

So Grendel became ruler; against right he fought,
one against all. Empty then stood
the best of houses, and for no brief space;
for twelve long winters torment sat
on the Friend of the Scyldings, fierce sorrows
and woes of every kind; which was not hidden
from the sons of men, but was made known
150   in grieving songs, how Grendel warred
long on Hrothgar, the harms he did him
through wretched years of wrong, outrage
and persecution. Peace was not in his mind
towards any companion of the court of Hrothgar,
the feud was not abated, the blood-price was unpaid.
Nor did any counsellor have cause to look for
a bright man-price at the murderer's hand:
the dark death-shadow drove always against them,
old and young; abominable
160   he watched and waited for them, walked nightlong
the misty moorland. Men know not
where hell's familiars fleet on their errands!

Again and again the enemy of man
stalking unseen, struck terrible
and bitter blows. In the black nights
he camped in the hall, under Heorot's gold roof;
yet he could not touch the treasure-throne
against the Lord's will, whose love was unknown to him.

A great grief was it for the Guardian of the Scyldings,
170 crushing to his spirit. The council lords
sat there daily to devise some plan,
what might be best for brave-hearted
Danes to contrive against these terror-raids.
They prayed aloud, promising sometimes
on the altars of their idols unholy sacrifices
if the Slayer of souls would send relief
to the suffering people.

                   Such was their practice,
a heathen hope; Hell possessed
their hearts and minds: the Maker was unknown to them,
180 the Judge of all actions, the Almighty was unheard of,
they knew not how to praise the Prince of Heaven,
the Wielder of Glory.

                Woe to him who must
in terrible trial entrust his soul
to the embrace of the burning, banished from thought
of change or comfort! Cheerful the man
able to look to the Lord at his death-day,
to find peace in the Father's embrace!
This season rocked the son of Healfdene
with swingeing sorrows; nor could the splendid man
190 put his cares from him. Too cruel the feud,
too strong and long-lasting, that struck that people,
a wicked affliction, the worst of nightmares!

This was heard of at his home by one of *Hygelac*'s
       followers,
a good man among the Geats, Grendel's raidings;
he was for main strength of all men foremost
that trod the earth at that time of day;

build and blood matched.

He bade a seaworthy
wave-cutter be fitted out for him; the warrior king
he would seek, he said, over swan's riding,
200   that lord of great name, needing men.
The wiser sought to dissuade him from voyaging
hardly or not at all, though they held him dear;
they whetted his quest-thirst, watched omens.
The prince had already picked his men
from the folk's flower, the fiercest among them
that might be found. With fourteen men
he sought sound-wood; sea-wise *Beowulf*
led them right down to the land's edge.

Time running on, she rode the waves now,
210   hard in by headland. Harnessed warriors
stepped on her stem; setting tide churned
sea with sand, soldiers carried
bright mail-coats to the mast's foot,
war-gear well-wrought; willingly they shoved her out,
thorough-braced craft, on the craved voyage.

Away she went over a wavy ocean,
boat like a bird, breaking seas,
wind-whetted, white-throated,
till the curved prow had ploughed so far
220   – the sun standing right on the second day –
that they might see land loom on the skyline,
then the shimmer of cliffs, sheer fells behind,
reaching capes.

The crossing was at an end;
closed the wake. Weather-Geats

stood on strand, stepped briskly up;
a rope going ashore, ring-mail clashed,
battle-girdings. God they thanked
for the smooth going over the salt trails.

The watchman saw them. From the wall where he stood,
230 posted by the Scyldings to patrol the cliffs,
he saw the polished lindens pass along the gangway
and the clean equipment. Curiosity
moved him to know who these men might be.

Hrothgar's thane, when his horse had picked
its way down to the shore, shook his spear
fiercely at arm's length, framed the challenge:
'Strangers, you have steered this steep craft
through the sea-ways, sought our coast.
I see you are warriors; you wear that dress now.
I must ask who you are.
240   In all the years
I have lived as look-out at land's end here
– so that no foreigners with a fleet-army
might land in Denmark and do us harm –
shield-carriers have never come ashore
more openly. You had no assurance
of welcome here, word of leave
from Hrothgar and *Hrothulf*!
                          I have not in my life
set eyes on a man with more might in his frame
than this helmed lord. He's no hall-fellow
250 dressed in fine armour, or his face belies him;
he has the head of a hero.
                          I'll have your names now

and the names of your fathers; or further you shall not go
as undeclared spies in the Danish land.
Stay where you are, strangers, hear
what I have to say! Seas crossed,
it is best and simplest straightaway to acknowledge
where you are from, why you have come.'

The captain gave him a clear answer,
leader of the troop, unlocked his word-hoard:
260 'We here are come from the country of the Geats
and are King Hygelac's hearth-companions.
My noble father was known as Edgetheow,
a front-fighter famous among nations,
who had seen many seasons when he set out at last
an old man from the halls; all the wiser men
in the world readily remember him.

It is with loyal and true intention that we come
to seek your lord the son of Healfdene,
guardian of the people: guide us well therefore!
270 We have a great errand to the glorious hero,
the Shepherd of the Danes; the drift of it
shall not be kept from you. You must know if indeed
there is truth in what is told in Geatland,
that among the Scyldings some enemy,
an obscure assailant in the opaque night-times,
makes spectacles of spoil and slaughter
in hideous feud. To Hrothgar I would
openheartedly unfold a plan
how the old commander may overcome his foe;
280 if indeed an easing is ever to slacken
these besetting sorrows, a settlement

when chafing cares shall cool at last.
Otherwise he must miserably live out
this lamentable time, for as long as Heorot,
best of houses, bulks to the sky.'

The mounted coastguard made reply,
unshrinking officer: 'A sharp-witted man,
clear in his mind, must be skilled
to discriminate deeds and words.
290 I accept what I am told, that this troop is loyal
to the Scyldings' Protector. Pass forward with your
weapons and war-dress! I am willing to guide you,
commanding meanwhile the men under me
to guard with care this craft of yours,
this new-tarred boat at its berth by our strand
against every enemy until again it bear
its beloved captain over the current sea,
curve-necked keel, to the coasts of the Geat;
such a warrior shall be accorded
300 unscathed passage through the shocks of battle.'

The vessel was still as they set forward,
the deep-chested ship, stayed at its mooring,
fast at its anchor. Over the cheek-pieces
boar-figures shone, bristling with gold,
blazing and fire-hard, fierce guards
of their bearers' lives. Briskly the men went
marching together, making out at last
the ample eaves adorned with gold:
to earth's men the most glorious
310 of houses under heaven, the home of the king;
its radiance lighted the lands of the world.

The coastguard showed them the shining palace,
the resort of heroes, and how they might
rightly come to it; this captain in the wars
then brought his horse about, and broke silence:
'Here I must leave you. May the Lord Almighty
afford His grace in your undertakings
and bring you to safety. Back at the sea-shore
I resume the watch against sea-raiders.'

320   There was stone paving on the path that brought
the war-band on its way. The war-coats shone
and the links of hard hand-locked iron
sang in their harness as they stepped along
in their gear of grim aspect, going to the hall.
Sea-wearied, they then set against the wall
their broad shields of special temper,
and bowed to bench, battle-shirts clinking,
the war-dress of warriors. The weapons of the seamen
stood in the spear-rack, stacked together,
330   an ash-wood grey-tipped. These iron-shirted men
were handsomely armed.

                  A high-mannered chieftain
then inquired after the ancestry of the warriors.
'From whence do you bring these embellished shields,
grey mail-shirts, masked helmets,
this stack of spears? I am spokesman here,
herald to Hrothgar; I have not seen
a body of strangers bear themselves more proudly.
It is not exile but adventure, I am thinking,
boldness of spirit, that brings you to Hrothgar.'

340 The gallant Geat gave answer then,
valour-renowned, and vaunting spoke,
hard under helmet: 'At Hygelac's table
we are sharers in the banquet; Beowulf is my name.
I shall gladly set out to the son of Healfdene,
most famous of kings, the cause of my journey,
lay it before your lord, if he will allow us kindly
to greet in person his most gracious self.'

Then Wulfgar spoke; the warlike spirit
of this Wendel prince, his wisdom in judgement,
350 were known to many. 'The Master of the Danes,
Lord of the Scyldings, shall learn of your request.
I shall gladly ask my honoured chief,
giver of arm-bands, about your undertaking,
and soon bear the answer back again to you
that my gracious lord shall think good to make.'

He strode rapidly to the seat of Hrothgar,
old and grey-haired among the guard of earls,
stepped forward briskly, stood before the shoulders
of the King of the Danes; a court's ways were known to
  him.
360 Then Wulfgar addressed his dear master:
'Men have come here from the country of the Geats,
borne from afar over the back of the sea;
these battle-companions call the man
who leads them, Beowulf. The boon they ask
is, my lord, that they may hold
converse with you. Do not, kind Hrothgar,
refuse them audience in the answer you vouchsafe;
accoutrement would clearly bespeak them

of earls' rank. Indeed the leader
370   who guided them here seems of great account.'

The Guardian of the Scyldings gave his answer:
'I knew him when he was a child!
It was to his old father, Edgetheow, that
Hrethel the Geat gave in marriage
his one daughter. Well does the son
now pay this call on a proven ally!

The seafarers used to say, I remember,
who took our gifts to the Geat people
in token of friendship – that this fighting man
380   in his hand's grasp had the strength
of thirty other men. I am thinking that
the Holy God, as a grace to us
Danes in the West, has directed him here
against Grendel's oppression. This good man shall be
offered treasures in return for his courage.

Waste no time now but tell them to come in
that they may see this company seated together.
Make sure to say that they are most welcome
to the people of the Danes.'
                    Promptly Wulfgar
390   turned to the doors and told his message:
'The Master of Battles bids me announce,
the Lord of the North Danes, that he knows your ancestry;
I am to tell you all, determined venturers
over the seas, that you are sure of welcome.
You may go in now in your gear of battle,
set eyes on Hrothgar, helmed as you are.

But battle-shafts and shields of linden wood
may here await your words' outcome.'

The prince arose, around him warriors
400 in dense escort; detailed by the chief,
a group remained to guard the weapons.
The Geats swung in behind their stout leader
over Heorot's floor. The hero led on,
hard under helmet, to the hearth, where he stopped.
Then Beowulf spoke; bent by smith's skill
the meshed rings of his mail-shirt glittered.
'Health to Hrothgar! I am Hygelac's kinsman
and serve in his fellowship. Fame-winning deeds
have come early to my hands. The affair of Grendel
410 has been made known to me on my native turf.
The sailors speak of this splendid hall,
this most stately building, standing idle
and silent of voices, as soon as the evening light
has hidden below the heaven's bright edge.
Whereupon it was urged by the ablest men
among our people, men proved in counsel,
that I should seek you out, most sovereign Hrothgar.
These men knew well the weight of my hands.
Had they not seen me come home from fights
420 where I had bound five Giants – their blood was upon me –
cleaned out a nest of them? Had I not crushed on the wave
sea-serpents by night in narrow struggle,
broken the beasts? (The bane of the Geats,
they had asked for their trouble.) And shall I not try
a single match with this monster Grendel,
a trial against this troll?
                To you I now

put one request, Royal Scylding,
Shield of the South Danes, one sole favour
that you'll not deny me, dear lord of your people,
430   now that I have come thus far, Fastness of Warriors;
that I alone may be allowed, with my loyal and
      determined
crew of companions, to cleanse your hall Heorot.

As I am informed that this unlovely one
is careless enough to carry no weapon,
so that my lord Hygelac, my leader in war,
may take joy in me, I abjure utterly
the bearing of sword or shielding yellow
board in this battle! With bare hands shall I
grapple with the fiend, fight to the death here,
440   hater and hated! He who is chosen
shall deliver himself to the Lord's judgement.

If he can contrive it, we may count upon Grendel
to eat quite fearlessly the flesh of Geats
here in this war-hall; has he not chewed
on the strength of this nation? There will be no need,
      Sir,
for you to bury my head; he will have me gladly,
if death should take me, though darkened with blood.
He will bear my bloody corpse away, bent on eating it,
make his meal alone, without misgiving,
450   bespatter his moor-lair. The disposing of my body
need occupy you no further then.
But if the fight should take me, you would forward to
      Hygelac
this best of battle-shirts, that my breast now wears.

The queen of war-coats, it is the bequest of Hrethel
and from the forge of Wayland. Fate will take its course!'

Then Hrothgar spoke, the Helmet of the Scyldings:
'So it is to fight in our defence, my friend Beowulf,
and as an office of kindness that you have come to us here!
Great was the feud that your father set off
460   when his hand struck down Heatholaf in death
among the Wylfings. The Weather-Geats
did not dare to keep him then, for dread of war,
and he left them to seek out the South-Danish folk,
the glorious Scyldings, across the shock of waters.
I had assumed sway over the Scylding nation
and in my youth ruled this rich kingdom,
storehouse of heroes. Heorogar was then dead,
the son of Healfdene had hastened from us,
my elder brother; a better man than I!
470   I then settled the feud with fitting payment,
sent to the Wylfings over the water's back
old things of beauty; against which I'd the oath of your
        father.

It is a sorrow in spirit for me to say to any man
– a grief in my heart – what the hatred of Grendel
has brought me to in Heorot, what humiliation,
what harrowing pain. My hall-companions,
my war-band, are dwindled; Weird has swept them
into the power of Grendel. Yet God could easily
check the ravages of this reckless fiend!
480   They often boasted, when the beer was drunk,
and called out over the ale-cup, my captains in battle,
that they would here await, in this wassailing-place,

with deadliness of iron edges, the onset of Grendel.
When morning brought the bright daylight
this mead-hall was seen all stained with blood:
blood had soaked its shining floor,
it was a house of slaughter. More slender grew my
strength of dear warriors; death took them off . . .
Yet sit now to the banquet, where you may soon attend,
490   should the mood so take you, some tale of victory.'

A bench was then cleared for the company of Geats
there in the beer-hall, for the whole band together.
The stout-hearted warriors went to their places,
bore their strength proudly. Prompt in his office,
the man who held the horn of bright mead
poured out its sweetness. The song of the poet
again rang in Heorot. The heroes laughed loud
in the great gathering of the Geats and the Danes.

Then *Unferth* spoke, the son of Edgelaf,
500   sitting at the feet of the Father of the Scyldings,
unbound a battle-rune. Beowulf's undertaking,
the seaman's bold venture, vexed him much.
He could not allow that another man
should hold under heaven a higher care
for wonders in the world than went with his own name.
'Is this the Beowulf of Breca's swimming-match,
who strove against him on the stretched ocean,
when for pride the pair of you proved the seas
and for a trite boast entrusted your lives
510   to the deep waters, undissuadable
by effort of friend or foe whatsoever
from that swimming on the sea? A sorry contest!

Your arms embraced the ocean's streams,
you beat the wave-way, wove your hand-movements,
and danced on the Spear-Man. The sea boiled with
       whelming
waves of winter; in the water's power
you laboured seven nights: and then you *lost* your
       swimming-match,
his might was the greater; morning found him
cast by the sea on the coast of the Battle-Reams.
520 He made his way back to the marches of the Brondings,
to his father-land, friend to his people,
and to the city-fastness where he had subjects, treasure
and his own stronghold. The son of Beanstan
performed to the letter what he had promised to you.
I see little hope then of a happier outcome
– though in other conflicts elsewhere in the world
you may indeed have prospered – if you propose
       awaiting
Grendel all night, on his own ground, unarmed.'

Then spoke Beowulf, son of Edgetheow:
530 'I thank my friend Unferth, who unlocks us this tale
of Breca's bragged exploit; the beer lends
eloquence to his tongue. But the truth is as I've said:
I had more sea-strength, outstaying Breca's,
and endured underwater a much worse struggle.

    It was in early manhood that we undertook
with a public boast – both of us still
very young men – to venture our lives
on the open ocean; which we accordingly did.
Hard in our right hands we held each a sword

540   as we went through the sea, so to keep off
the whales from us. If he whitened the ocean,
no wider appeared the water between us.
He could not away from me; nor would I from him.
Thus stroke for stroke we stitched the ocean
five nights and days, drawn apart then
by cold storm on the cauldron of waters;
under lowering night the northern wind
fell on us in warspite: the waves were rough!

      The unfriendliness was then aroused of the fishes of the
          deep.

550   Against sea-beasts my body-armour,
hand-linked and hammered, helped me then,
this forge-knit battleshirt bright with gold,
decking my breast. Down to the bottom
I was plucked in rage by this reptile-fish,
pinned in his grip. But I got the chance
to thrust once at the ugly creature
with my weapon's point: war took off then
the mighty monster; mine was the hand did it.
Then loathsome snouts snickered by me,
560   swarmed at my throat. I served them out
with my good sword, gave them what they asked for:
those scaly flesh-eaters sat not down
to dine on Beowulf, they browsed not on me
in that picnic they'd designed in the dingles of the sea.
Daylight found them dispersed instead
up along the beaches where my blade had laid them
soundly asleep; since then they have never
troubled the passage of travellers over
that deep water-way. Day in the east grew,

570   God's bright beacon, and the billows sank
so that I then could see the headlands,
the windy cliffs. "Weird saves oft
the man undoomed if he undaunted be!" –
and it was my part then to put to the sword
nine sea-monsters, in the severest fight
by night I have heard of under heaven's vault;
a man more sorely pressed the seas never held.
I came with my life from the compass of my foes,
but tired from the struggle. The tide bore me
580   away on its currents to the coasts of Norway,
whelms of water.

                    No whisper has yet reached me
of sword-ambushes survived, nor such scathing perils
in connection with your name! Never has Breca,
nor you Unferth either, in open battle-play
framed such a deed of daring with your
shining swords – small as my action was.
You have killed only kindred, kept your blade
for those closest in blood; you're a clever man, Unferth,
but you'll endure hell's damnation for that.

590   It speaks for itself, my son of Edgelaf,
that Grendel had never grown such a terror,
this demon had never dealt your lord
such havoc in Heorot, had your heart's intention
been so grim for battle as you give us to believe.
He's learnt there's in fact not the least need
excessively to respect the spite of this people,
the scathing steel-thresh of the Scylding nation.
He spares not a single sprig of your Danes
in extorting his tribute, but treats himself proud,

600   butchering and dispatching, and expects no resistance
from the spear-wielding Scyldings.

                     I'll show him Geatish
strength and stubbornness shortly enough now,
a lesson in war. He who wishes shall go then
blithe to the banquet when the breaking light
of another day shall dawn for men
and the sun shine glorious in the southern sky.'

Great then was the hope of the grey-locked Hrothgar,
warrior, giver of rings. Great was the trust
of the Shield of the Danes, shepherd of the people,
610   attending to Beowulf's determined resolve.

There was laughter of heroes, harp-music ran,
words were warm-hearted. *Wealhtheow* moved,
mindful of courtesies, the queen of Hrothgar,
glittering to greet the Geats in the hall,
peerless lady; but to the land's guardian
she offered first the flowing cup,
bade him be blithe at the beer-drinking,
gracious to his people; gladly the conqueror
partook of the banquet, tasted the hall-cup.
620   The Helming princess then passed about among
the old and the young men in each part of the hall,
bringing the treasure-cup, until the time came
when the flashing-armed queen, complete in all virtues,
carried out to Beowulf the brimming vessel;
she greeted the Geat, and gave thanks to the Lord
in words wisely chosen, her wish being granted
to meet with a man who might be counted on
for aid against these troubles. He took then the cup,

a man violent in war, at Wealhtheow's hand,
630 and framed his utterance, eager for the conflict.

Thus spoke Beowulf son of Edgetheow:
'This was my determination in taking to the ocean,
benched in the ship among my band of fellows,
that I should once and for all accomplish the wishes
of your adopted people, or pass to the slaughter,
viced in my foe's grip. This vow I shall accomplish,
a deed worthy of an earl; decided otherwise
here in this mead-hall to meet my ending-day!'

This speech sounded sweet to the lady,
640 the vaunt of the Geat; glittering she moved
to her lord's side, splendid folk-queen.

Then at last Heorot heard once more
words of courage, the carousing of a people
singing their victories; till the son of Healfdene
desired at length to leave the feast,
be away to his night's rest; aware of the monster
brooding his attack on the tall-gabled hall
from the time they had seen the sun's lightness
to the time when darkness drowns everything
650 and under its shadow-cover shapes do glide
dark beneath the clouds. The company came to its feet.

Then did the heroes, Hrothgar and Beowulf,
salute each other; success he wished him,
control of the wine-hall, and with this word left him:
'Never since I took up targe and sword
have I at any instance to any man beside,

thus handed over Heorot, as I here do to you.
Have and hold now the house of the Danes!
Bend your mind and your body to this task
660   and wake against the foe! There'll be no want of
        liberality
if you come out alive from this ordeal of courage.'
Then Hrothgar departed, the Protector of the Danes
passed from the hall at the head of his troop.
The war-leader sought Wealhtheow his queen,
the companion of his bed.

                Thus did the King of Glory,
to oppose this Grendel, appoint a hall-guard
– so the tale went abroad – who took on a special
task at the court – to cope with the monster.
The Geat prince placed all his trust
670   in his mighty strength, his Maker's favour.

He now uncased himself of his coat of mail,
unhelmed his head, handed his attendant
his embellished sword, best of weapons,
and bade him take care of these trappings of war.
Beowulf then made a boasting speech,
the Geat man, before mounting his bed:
'I fancy my fighting-strength, my performance in combat,
at least as greatly as Grendel does his;
and therefore I shall not cut short his life
680   with a slashing sword – too simple a business.
He has not the art to answer me in kind,
hew at my shield, shrewd though he be
at his nasty catches. No, we'll at night play
without any weapons – if unweaponed he dare
to face me in fight. The Father in His wisdom

shall apportion the honours then, the All-holy Lord,
to whichever side shall seem to Him fit.'

Then the hero lay down, leant his head
on the bolster there; about him many
690   brave sea-warriors bowed to their hall-rest.
Not one of them thought he would thence be departing
ever to set eyes on his own country,
the home that nourished him, or its noble people;
for they had heard how many men of the Danes
death had dragged from that drinking-hall.
But God was to grant to the Geat people
the clue to war-success in the web of fate –
His help and support; so that they did
overcome the foe – through the force of one
700   unweaponed man. The Almighty Lord
has ruled the affairs of the race of men
thus from the beginning.
                                        Gliding through the shadows came
the walker in the night; the warriors slept
whose task was to hold the horned building,
all except one. It was well-known to men
that the demon could not drag them to the shades
without God's willing it; yet the one man kept
unblinking watch. He awaited, heart swelling
with anger against his foe, the ordeal of battle.
710   Down off the moorlands' misting fells came
Grendel stalking; God's brand was on him.
The spoiler meant to snatch away
from the high hall some of human race.
He came on under the clouds, clearly saw at last
the gold-hall of men, the mead-drinking place

nailed with gold plates. That was not the first visit
he had paid to the hall of Hrothgar the Dane:
he never before and never after
harder luck nor hall-guards found.

720 Walking to the hall came this warlike creature
condemned to agony. The door gave way,
toughened with iron, at the touch of those hands.
Rage-inflamed, wreckage-bent, he ripped open
the jaws of the hall. Hastening on,
the foe then stepped onto the unstained floor,
angrily advanced: out of his eyes stood
an unlovely light like that of fire.
He saw then in the hall a host of young soldiers,
a company of kinsmen caught away in sleep,
730 a whole warrior-band. In his heart he laughed then,
horrible monster, his hopes swelling
to a gluttonous meal. He meant to wrench
the life from each body that lay in the place
before night was done. It was not to be;
he was no longer to feast on the flesh of mankind
after that night.
                    Narrowly the powerful
kinsman of Hygelac kept watch how the ravager
set to work with his sudden catches;
nor did the monster mean to hang back.
740 As a first step he set his hands on
a sleeping soldier, savagely tore at him,
gnashed at his bone-joints, bolted huge gobbets,
sucked at his veins, and had soon eaten
all of the dead man, even down to his
hands and feet.

Forward he stepped,
stretched out his hands to seize the warrior
calmly at rest there, reached out for him with his
unfriendly fingers: but the faster man
forestalling, sat up, sent back his arm.
750   The upholder of evils at once knew
he had not met, on middle earth's
extremest acres, with any man
of harder hand-grip: his heart panicked.
He was quit of the place no more quickly for that.

Eager to be away, he ailed for his darkness
and the company of devils; the dealings he had there
were like nothing he had come across in his lifetime.
Then Hygelac's brave kinsman called to mind
that evening's utterance, upright he stood,
760   fastened his hold till fingers were bursting.
The monster strained away: the man stepped closer.
The monster's desire was for darkness between them,
direction regardless, to get out and run
for his fen-bordered lair; he felt his grip's strength
crushed by his enemy. It was an ill journey
the rough marauder had made to Heorot.

The crash in the banqueting-hall came to the Danes,
the men of the guard that remained in the buildings,
with the taste of death. The deepening rage
770   of the claimants to Heorot caused it to resound.
It was indeed wonderful that the wine-supper-hall
withstood the wrestling pair, that the world's palace
fell not to the ground. But it was girt firmly,
both inside and out, by iron braces

of skilled manufacture. Many a figured
gold-worked wine-bench, as we heard it,
started from the floor at the struggles of that pair.
The men of the Danes had not imagined that
any of mankind by what method soever
780   might undo that intricate, antlered hall,
sunder it by strength – unless it were swallowed up in
the embraces of fire.
                    Fear entered into
the listening North Danes, as that noise rose up again
strange and strident. It shrilled terror
to the ears that heard it through the hall's side-wall,
the grisly plaint of God's enemy,
his song of ill-success, the sobs of the damned one
bewailing his pain. He was pinioned there
by the man of all mankind living
790   in this world's estate the strongest of his hands.

Not for anything would the earls' guardian
let his deadly guest go living:
he did not count his continued existence
of the least use to anyone. The earls ran
to defend the person of their famous prince;
they drew their ancestral swords to bring
what aid they could to their captain, Beowulf.
They were ignorant of this, when they entered the fight,
boldly-intentioned battle-friends,
800   to hew at Grendel, hunt his life
on every side – that no sword on earth,
not the truest steel, could touch their assailant;
for by a spell he had dispossessed all
blades of their bite on him.

                              A bitter parting
from life was that day destined for him;
the eldritch spirit was sent off on his
far faring into the fiends' domain.

It was then that this monster, who, moved by spite
against human kind, had caused so much harm
810 – so feuding with God – found at last
that flesh and bone were to fail him in the end;
for Hygelac's great-hearted kinsman
had him by the hand; and hateful to each
was the breath of the other.
                              A breach in the giant
flesh-frame showed then, shoulder-muscles
sprang apart, there was a snapping of tendons,
bone-locks burst. To Beowulf the glory
of this fight was granted; Grendel's lot
to flee the slopes fen-ward with flagging heart,
820 to a den where he knew there could be no relief,
no refuge for a life at its very last stage,
whose surrender-day had dawned. The Danish hopes
in this fatal fight had found their answer.

He had cleansed Heorot. He who had come from afar,
deep-minded, strong-hearted, had saved the hall
from persecution. He was pleased with his night's work,
the deed he had done. Before the Danish people
the Geat captain had made good his boast,
had taken away all their unhappiness,
830 the evil menace under which they had lived,
enduring it by dire constraint,
no slight affliction. As a signal to all

the hero hung up the hand, the arm
and torn-off shoulder, the entire limb,
Grendel's whole grip, below the gable of the roof.

There was, as I heard it, at hall next morning
a great gathering in the gift-hall yard
to see the wonder. Along the wide highroads
the chiefs of the clans came from near and far
840   to see the foe's footprints. It may fairly be said
that his parting from life aroused no pity in any
who tracked the spoor-blood of his blind flight
for the monsters' mere-pool; with mood flagging
and strength crushed, he had staggered onwards;
each step evidenced his ebbing life's blood.
The tarn was troubled; a terrible wave-thrash
brimmed it, bubbling; black-mingled,
the warm wound-blood welled upwards.
He had dived to his doom, he had died miserably;
850   here in his fen-lair he had laid aside
his heathen soul. Hell welcomed it.

Then the older retainers turned back on the way
journeyed with much joy; joined by the young men,
the warriors on white horses wheeled away from the Mere
in bold mood. Beowulf's feat
was much spoken of, and many said,
that between the seas, south or north,
over earth's stretch no other man
beneath the sky's shifting excelled Beowulf,
860   of all who wielded the sword he was worthiest to rule.
In saying this they did not slight in the least
the gracious Hrothgar, for he was a good king.

Where, as they went, their way broadened
they would match their mounts, making them leap
along the best stretches, the strife-eager
on their fallow horses. Or a fellow of the king's,
whose head was a storehouse of the storied verse,
whose tongue gave gold to the language
of the treasured repertory, wrought a new lay
870   made in the measure. The man struck up,
found the phrase, framed rightly
the deed of Beowulf, drove the tale,
rang word-changes.

                 Of Wæls's great son,
Sigemund, he spoke then, spelling out to them
all he had heard of that hero's strife,
his fights, strange feats, far wanderings,
the feuds and the blood spilt. Fitela alone heard
these things not well nor widely known to men,
when Sigemund chose to speak in this vein
880   to his sister's son. They were inseparable
in every fight, the firmest of allies;
their swords had between them scythed to the ground
a whole race of monsters. The reputation
that spread at his death was no slight one:
Sigemund it was who had slain the dragon,
the keeper of the hoard; the king's son walked
under the grey rock, he risked alone
that fearful conflict; Fitela was not there.
Yet it turned out well for him, his weapon transfixed
890   the marvellous snake, struck in the cave-wall,
best of swords; the serpent was dead.
Sigemund's valour had so prevailed
that the whole ring-hoard was his to enjoy,

dispose of as he wished. Wæls's great son
loaded his ship with shining trophies,
stacking them by the mast; the monster shrivelled away.
He was by far the most famous of adventurers
among the peoples, this protector of warriors,
for the deeds by which he had distinguished himself.

900 *Heremod*'s stature and strength had decayed then,
his daring diminished. Deeply betrayed
into the fiends' power, far among the Giants
he was done to death. Dark sorrows
drove him mad at last. A deadly grief
he had become to his people and the princes of his land.
Wise men among the leaders had lamented that career,
their fierce one's fall, who in former days
had looked to him for relief of their ills,
hoping that their lord's son would live and in ripeness
910 assume the kingdom, the care of his people,
the hoard and the stronghold, the storehouse of heroes,
the Scylding homeland. Whereas Hygelac's kinsman
endeared himself ever more deeply to friends
and to all mankind, evil seized Heremod.

The riders returning came racing their horses
along dusty-pale roads. The dawn had grown
into broadest day, and, drawn by their eagerness
to see the strange sight, there had assembled at the hall
many keen warriors. The king himself,
920 esteemed for excellence, stepped glorious
from his wife's chambers, the warden of ring-hoards,
with much company; and his queen walked
the mead-path by him, her maidens following.

34

Taking his stand on the steps of the hall,
Hrothgar beheld the hand of Grendel
below the gold gable-end; and gave speech:
'Let swift thanks be given to the Governor of All,
seeing this sight! I have suffered a thousand
spites from Grendel: but God works ever
930   miracle upon miracle, the Master of Heaven.
Until yesterday I doubted whether
our afflictions would find a remedy
in my lifetime, since this loveliest of halls
stood slaughter-painted, spattered with blood.
For all my counsellors this was a cruel sorrow,
for none of them imagined they could mount a defence
of the Scylding stronghold against such enemies –
warlocks, demons!
                But one man has,
by the Lord's power, performed the thing
940   that all our thought and arts to this day
had failed to do. She may indeed say,
whoever she be that brought into the world
this young man here – if yet she lives –
that the God of Old was gracious to her
in her child-bearing. Beowulf, I now take you
to my bosom as a son, O best of men,
and cherish you in my heart. Hold yourself well
in this new relation! You will lack for nothing
that lies in my gift of the goods of this world:
950   lesser offices have elicited reward,
we have honoured from our hoard less heroic men,
far weaker in war. But you have well ensured
by the deeds of your hands an undying honour

for your name for ever. May the Almighty Father
yield you always the success that you yesternight
enjoyed!'

Beowulf spoke, son of Edgetheow:
'We willingly undertook this test of courage,
risked a match with the might of the stranger,
and performed it all. I would prefer, though,
960   that you had rather seen the rest of him here,
the whole length of him, lying here dead.
I had meant to catch him, clamp him down
with a cruel lock to his last resting-place;
with my hands upon him, I would have him soon
in the throes of death – unless he disappeared!
But I had not a good enough grip to prevent
his getting away, when God did not wish it;
the fiend in his flight was far too violent,
my life's enemy. But he left his hand
970   behind him here, so as to have his life,
and his arm and shoulder. And all for nothing:
it bought him no respite, wretched creature.
He lives no longer, laden with sins,
to plague mankind: pain has set
heavy hands on him, and hasped about him
fatal fetters. He is forced to await now,
like a guilty criminal, a greater judgement,
where the Lord in His splendour shall pass sentence
upon him.'

The son of Edgelaf was more silent then
980   in boasting of his own battle-deeds:
the athelings gazed at what the earl's strength

had hung there – the hand, high up under the roof,
and the fingers of their foe. From the front, each one
of the socketed nails seemed steel to the eye,
each spur on the hand of that heathen warrior
a terrible talon. They told each other
nothing could be hard enough to harm it at all,
not the most ancient of iron swords
would bite on that bloody battle-hand.

990 Other hands were pressed then to prepare the inside
of the banqueting-hall, and briskly too.
Many were ready, both men and women,
to adorn the guest-hall. Gold-embroidered tapestries
glowed from the walls, with wonderful sights
for every creature that cared to look at them.
The bright building had badly started
in all its inner parts, despite its iron bands,
and the hinges were ripped off. Only the roof survived
unmarred and in one piece when the monstrous one,
1000 flecked with his crimes, had fled the place
in despair of his life.
                              But to elude death
is not easy: attempt it who will,
he shall go to the place prepared for each
of the sons of men, the soul-bearers
dwelling on earth, ordained them by fate:
laid fast in that bed, the body shall sleep
when the feast is done.
                              In due season
the king himself came to the hall;
Healfdene's son would sit at the banquet.
1010 No people has gathered in greater retinue,

borne themselves better about their ring-giver.
Men known for their courage came to the benches,
rejoiced in the feast; they refreshed themselves kindly
with many a mead-cup; in their midst the brave kinsmen,
father's brother and brother's son,
Hrothgar and Hrothulf. Heorot's floor was
filled with friends: falsity in those days
had no place in the dealings of the Danish people.

Then as a sign of victory the son of Healfdene
1020　bestowed on Beowulf a standard worked in gold,
a figured battle-banner, breast and head-armour;
and many admired the marvellous sword
that was borne before the hero. Beowulf drank with
the company in the hall. He had no cause to be ashamed of
gifts so fine before the fighting-men!
I have not heard that many men at arms
have given four such gifts of treasure
more openly to another at the mead.
At the crown of the helmet, the head-protector,
1030　was a rim, with wire wound round it, to stop
the file-hardened blade that fights have tempered
from shattering it, when the shield-warrior
must go out against grim enemies.

The king then ordered eight war-horses
with glancing bridles to be brought within walls
and onto the floor. Fretted with gold
and studded with stones was one saddle there!
This was the battle-seat of the Bulwark of the Danes,
when in the sword-play the son of Healfdene
1040　would take his part; the prowess of the king

had never failed at the front where the fighting was mortal.
The Protector of the Sons of Scyld then gave
both to Beowulf, bidding him take care
to use them well, both weapons and horses.
Thus did the glorious prince, guardian of the treasure,
reward these deeds, with both war-horses and armour;
of such open-handedness no honest man
could ever speak in disparagement.

Then the lord of men also made a gift
1050 of treasure to each who had adventured with Beowulf
over the sea's paths, seated now at the benches –
an old thing of beauty. He bade compensation
to be made too, in gold, for the man whom Grendel
had horribly murdered; more would have gone
had not the God overseeing us, and the resolve of a man,
stood against that weird. The Wielder guided then
the dealings of mankind, as He does even now.
A mind that seeks to understand and grasp this
is therefore best. Both bad and good,
1060 and much of both, must be borne in a lifetime
spent on this earth in these anxious days.

Then string and song sounded together
before Healfdene's Helper-in-battle:
the lute was taken up and tales recited
when Hrothgar's bard was bidden to sing
a hall-song for the men on the mead-benches.
It was how disaster came to the sons of *Finn*:
first the Half-Dane champion, *Hnæf* of the Scyldings,
was fated to fall in the Frisian ambush.
1070 *Hildeburgh* their lady had little cause to speak

of the good faith of the Jutes; guiltless she had suffered
in that linden-wood clash the loss of her closest ones,
her son and her brother, both born to die there,
struck down by the spear. Sorrowful princess!
This decree of fate the daughter of Hoc
mourned with good reason; for when morning came
the clearness of heaven disclosed to her
the murder of those kindred who were the cause of all
her earthly bliss.

                    Battle had also claimed
1080 all but a few of Finn's retainers
in that place of assembly; he was unable therefore
to bring to a finish the fight with *Hengest*,
force out and crush the few survivors
of Hnæf's troop. The truce-terms they put to him
were that he should make over a mead-hall to the Danes,
with high-seat and floor; half of it
to be held by them, half by the Jutes.
In sharing out goods, that the son of Folcwalda
should every day give honour to the Danes
1090 of Hengest's party, providing rings
and prizes from the hoard, plated with gold,
treating them identically in the drinking-hall
as when he chose to cheer his own Frisians.
On both sides they then bound themselves fast
in a pact of friendship. Finn then swore
strong unexceptioned oaths to Hengest
to hold in honour, as advised by his counsellors,
the battle-survivors; similarly no man
by word or deed to undo the pact,
1100 as by mischievous cunning to make complaint of it,
despite that they were serving the slayer of their prince,

since their lordless state so constrained them to do;
but that if any Frisian should fetch the feud to mind
and by taunting words awaken the bad blood,
it should be for the sword's edge to settle it then.

The pyre was erected, the ruddy gold
brought from the hoard, and the best warrior
of Scylding race was ready for the burning.
Displayed on his pyre, plain to see
1110   were the bloody mail-shirt, the boars on the helmets,
iron-hard, gold-clad; and gallant men about him
all marred by their wounds; mighty men had fallen there.
Hildeburgh then ordered her own son
to be given to the funeral fire of Hnæf
for the burning of his bones; bade him be laid
at his uncle's side. She sang the dirges,
bewailed her grief. The warrior went up;
the greatest of corpse-fires coiled to the sky,
roared before the mounds. There were melting heads
1120   and bursting wounds, as the blood sprang out
from weapon-bitten bodies. Blazing fire,
most insatiable of spirits, swallowed the remains
of the victims of both nations. Their valour was no more.

The warriors then scattered and went to their homes.
Missing their comrades, they made for Friesland,
the home and high stronghold. But Hengest still,
as he was constrained to do, stayed with Finn
a death-darkened winter in dreams of his homeland.
He was prevented from passage of the sea
1130   in his ring-beaked boat: the boiling ocean
fought with the wind; winter locked the seas

in his icy binding; until another year
came at last to the dwellings, as it does still,
continually keeping its season,
the weather of rainbows.

                Now winter had fled
and earth's breast was fair, the exile strained
to leave these lodgings; yet it was less the voyage
that exercised his mind than the means of his vengeance,
the bringing about of the bitter conflict
1140 that he meditated for the men of the Jutes.
So he did not decline the accustomed remedy,
when the son of Hunlaf set across his knees
that best of blades, his battle-gleaming sword;
the Jutes were acquainted with the edges of that steel.

And so, in his hall, at the hands of his enemies,
Finn received the fatal sword-thrust;
Guthlaf and Oslaf, after the sea-crossing,
proclaimed their tribulations, their treacherous
          entertainment,
and named the author of them; anger in the breast
1150 rose irresistible. Red was the hall then
with the lives of foemen. Finn was slain there,
the king among his troop, and the queen taken.
The Scylding crewmen carried to the ship
the hall-furnishings of Friesland's king,
all they could find at Finnsburh
in gemstones and jewelwork. Journeying back,
they returned to the Danes their true-born lady,
restored her to her people.

                Thus the story was sung,
the gleeman's lay. Gladness mounted,

1160   bench-mirth rang out, the bearers gave
      wine from wonderful vessels. Then came Wealhtheow
           forward,
      going with golden crown to where the great heroes
      were sitting, uncle and nephew; their bond was sound at
           that time,
      each was true to the other. Likewise Unferth the
          spokesman
      sat at the footstool of Hrothgar. All had faith in his spirit,
      accounted his courage great – though toward his kinsmen
          he had not been
      kind at the clash of swords.
                        The Scylding queen then spoke:
      'Accept this cup, my king and lord,
      giver of treasure. Let your gaiety be shown,
1170   gold-friend of warriors, and to the Geats speak
      in words of friendship, for this well becomes a man.
      Be gracious to these Geats, and let the gifts you have had
      from near and far, not be forgotten now.

      I hear it is your wish to hold this warrior
      henceforward as your son. Heorot is cleansed,
      the ring-hall bright again: therefore bestow while you may
      these blessings liberally, and leave to your kinsmen
      the land and its people when your passing is decreed,
      your meeting with fate. For may I not count
1180   on my gracious Hrothulf to guard honourably
      our young ones here, if you, my lord,
      should give over this world earlier than he?
      I am sure that he will show to our children
      answerable kindness, if he keeps in remembrance

all that we have done to indulge and advance him,
the honours we bestowed on him when he was still a child.'

Then she turned to the bench where her boys were sitting,
Hrethric and Hrothmund, among the heroes' sons,
young men together; where the good man sat also
1190 between the two brothers, Beowulf the Geat.
Then the cup was taken to him and he was entreated
      kindly
to honour their feast; ornate gold
was presented in trophy: two arm-wreaths,
with robes and rings also, and the richest collar
I have ever heard of in all the world.

Never under heaven have I heard of a finer
prize among heroes – since Hama carried off
the Brising necklace to his bright city,
that gold-cased jewel; he gave the slip
1200 to the machinations of Eormenric, and made his name
      forever.

This gold was to be on the neck of the grandson of
      Swerting
on the last of his harryings, Hygelac the Geat,
as he stood before the standard astride his plunder,
defending his war-haul: Weird struck him down;
in his superb pride he provoked disaster
in the Frisian feud. This fabled collar
the great war-king wore when he crossed
the foaming waters; he fell beneath his shield.
The king's person passed into Frankish hands,
1210 together with his corselet, and this collar also.

They were lesser men that looted the slain;
for when the carnage was over, the corpse-field was littered
with the people of the Geats.
                       Applause filled the hall;
then Wealhtheow spoke, and her words were attended.

'Take pride in this jewel, have joy of this mantle
drawn from our treasuries, most dear Beowulf!
May fortune come with them and may you flourish in your
        youth!
Proclaim your strength; but in counsel to these boys
be a gentle guardian, and my gratitude will be seen.
1220 Already you have so managed that men everywhere
will hold you in honour for all time,
even to the cliffs at the world's end, washed by Ocean,
the wind's range. All the rest of your life
must be happy, prince; and prosperity I wish you too,
abundance of treasure! But be to my son
a friend in deed, most favoured of men.
You see how open is each earl here with his neighbour,
temperate of heart, and true to his lord.
The nobles are loyal, the lesser people dutiful;
1230 wine mellows the men to move to my bidding.'

She walked back to her place. What a banquet that was!
The men drank their wine: the weird they did not know,
destined from of old, the doom that was to fall
on many of the earls there. When evening came
Hrothgar departed to his private bower,
the king to his couch; countless were the men
who watched over the hall, as they had often done before.
They cleared away the benches, and covered the floor

with beds and bolsters: the best at the feast
1240 bent to his hall-rest, hurried to his doom.
Each by his head placed his polished shield,
the lindens of battle. On the benches aloft,
above each atheling, easily to be seen,
were the ring-stitched mail-coat, the mighty helmet
steepling above the fray, and the stout spear-shaft.
It was their habit always, at home or on campaign,
to be ready for war, in whichever case,
whatsoever the hour might be
that the need came on their lord: what a nation they were!

1250 Then they sank into sleep. A savage penalty
one paid for his night's rest! It was no new thing for that
          people
since Grendel had occupied the gold-giving hall,
working his evil, until the end came,
death for his misdeeds. It was declared then to men,
and received by every ear, that for all this time
a survivor had been living, an avenger for their foe
and his grim life's-leaving: *Grendel's Mother* herself,
a monstrous ogress, was ailing for her loss.
She had been doomed to dwell in the dread waters,
1260 in the chilling currents, because of that blow
whereby Cain became the killer of his brother,
his own father's son. He stole away, branded,
marked for his murder, from all that men delight in,
to inhabit the wastelands.
                    Hosts of the ill ones
sprang from his begetting; as Grendel, that hateful
accursed outcast, who encountered at Heorot
a watchful man waiting for the fight.

The grim one fastened his grip upon him there,
but he remembered his mighty strength,
1270   the gift that the Lord had so largely bestowed on him,
and, putting his faith in the favour of the Almighty
and His aid and comfort, he overcame the foe,
put down the hell-fiend. How humbling was that flight
when the miserable outcast crept to his dying-place!
Thus mankind's enemy. But his Mother now purposed
to set out at last — savage in her grief —
on that wrath-bearing visit of vengeance for her son.

She came down to Heorot, where the heroes of the Danes
slept about the hall. A sudden change
1280   was that for the men there when the Mother of Grendel
found her way in among them — though the fury of her
        onslaught
was less frightful than his; as the force of a woman,
her onset in a fight, is less feared by men,
where the bound blade, beaten out by hammers,
cuts, with its sharp edges shining with blood,
through the boars that bristle above the foes' helmets!

Many a hard sword was snatched up in the hall
from its rack above the benches; the broad shield was
        raised,
held in the hand firm; helmet and corselet
1290   lay there unheeded when the horror was on them.
She was all eager to be out of the place
now that she was discovered, and escape with her life.
She caught a man quickly, clutched him to herself,
one of the athelings, and was away to the fen.
This was the hero that Hrothgar loved better

than any on earth among his retinue,
destroyed thus as he slept; he was a strong warrior,
noted in battle. (Beowulf was not there:
separate lodging had been assigned that night,
1300 after the treasure-giving, to the Geat champion.)
Heorot was in uproar; the hand had gone with her,
blood-stained, familiar.
                  And so a fresh sorrow
came again to those dwellings. It was an evil bargain,
with both parties compelled to barter
the lives of their dearest. What disturbance of spirit
for the wise king, the white-haired soldier,
hearing the news that the nearest of his thanes
was dead and gone, his dearest man!

Beowulf was soon summoned to the chamber,
1310 victory-blest man. And that valiant warrior
came with his following – it was at first light –
captain of his company, to where the king waited
to see if by some means the Swayer of All
would work a turning into this tale of sorrow.
The man excellent in warfare walked across the hall
flanked by his escort – the floor-timbers boomed –
to make his addresses to the Danish lord,
the Guide of the Ingwine. He inquired of him whether
the night had been quiet, after a call so urgent.

1320 Hrothgar spoke, the Helmet of the Scyldings:
'Do not ask about our welfare! Woe has returned
to the Danish people with the death of *Ashhere*,
the elder brother of Yrmenlaf.

He was my closest counsellor, he was keeper of my
    thoughts,
he stood at my shoulder when we struck for our lives
at the crashing together of companies of foot,
when blows rained on boar-crests. Men of birth and
    merit
all should be as Ashhere was!
A bloodthirsty monster has murdered him in Heorot,
1330 a wandering demon; whither this terrible one,
glorying in her prey, glad of her meal,
has returned to, I know not. She has taken vengeance
for the previous night, when you put an end to Grendel
with forceful finger-grasp, and in a fierce manner,
because he had diminished and destroyed my people
for far too long. He fell in that struggle
and forfeited his life; but now is followed by another
most powerful ravager. Revenge is her motive,
and in furthering her son's feud she has gone far enough,
1340 – or thanes may be found who will think it so;
in their breasts they will grieve for their giver of rings,
bitter at heart. For the hand is stilled
that would openly have granted your every desire.

    I have heard it said by subjects of mine
who live in the country, counsellors in this hall,
that they have seen such a pair
of huge wayfarers haunting the moors,
otherworldly ones; and one of them,
so far as they might make it out,
1350 was in woman's shape; but the shape of a man,
though twisted, trod also the tracks of exile
– save that he was more huge than any human being.

The country people have called him from of old
by the name of Grendel; they know of no father for him,
nor whether there have been such beings before
among the monster-race.

                Mysterious is the region
they live in – of wolf-fells, wind-picked moors
and treacherous fen-paths: a torrent of water
pours down dark cliffs and plunges into the earth,
1360 an underground flood. It is not far from here,
in terms of miles, that the Mere lies,
overcast with dark, crag-rooted trees
that hang in groves hoary with frost.
An uncanny sight may be seen at night there
– the fire in the water! The wit of living men
is not enough to know its bottom.
The hart that roams the heath, when hounds have pressed
      him
long and hard, may hide in the forest
his antlered head; but the hart will die there
1370 sooner than swim and save his life;
he will sell it on the brink there, for it is not a safe place.
And the wind can stir up wicked storms there,
whipping the swirling waters up
till they climb the clouds and clog the air,
making the skies weep.

                Our sole remedy
is to turn again to you. The treacherous country
where that creature of sin is to be sought out
is strange to you as yet: seek then if you dare!
I shall reward the deed, as I did before,
1380 with wealthy gifts of wreathèd ore,
treasures from the hoard, if you return once more.'

Beowulf spoke, son of Edgetheow:
'Bear your grief, wise one! It is better for a man
to avenge his friend than to refresh his sorrow.
As we must all expect to leave
our life on this earth, we must earn some renown,
if we can, before death; daring is the thing
for a fighting man to be remembered by.

 Let Denmark's lord arise, and we shall rapidly see then
1390 where this kinswoman of Grendel's has gone away to!
I can promise you this, that she'll not protect herself by
   hiding
in any fold of the field, in any forest of the mountain,
in any dingle of the sea, dive where she will!
For this day, therefore, endure all your woes
with the patience that I may expect of you.'

The ancient arose and offered thanks to God,
to the Lord Almighty, for what this man had spoken.
A steed with braided mane was bridled then,
a horse for Hrothgar; the hero-patriarch
1400 rode out shining; shieldbearers marched
in troop beside him. The trace of her going
on the woodland paths was plainly to be seen,
stepping onwards; straight across
the fog-bound moor she had fetched away there
the lifeless body of the best man
of all who kept the courts of Hrothgar.
The sons of men then made their way
up steep screes, by scant tracks
where only one might walk, by wall-faced cliffs,
1410 through haunted fens – uninhabitable country.

Going on ahead with a handful of the
keener men to reconnoitre,
Beowulf suddenly saw where some ash-trees
hung above a hoary rock
— a cheerless wood! And the water beneath it
was turbid with blood; bitter distress
was to be endured by the Danes who were there,
a grief for the earls, for every thane
of the Friends of the Scyldings, when they found there
1420 the head of Ashhere by the edge of the cliff.

The men beheld the blood on the water,
its warm upwellings. The war-horn sang
an eager battle-cry. The band of foot-soldiers,
sitting by the water, could see multitudes
of strange sea-drakes swerving through the depths,
and water-snakes lay on the ledges of the cliffs,
such serpents and wild beasts as will sally out
in middle morning to make havoc
in the seas where ships sail.
                Slithering away
1430 at the bright phrases of the battle-horn,
they were swollen with anger. An arrow from the
bow of Beowulf broke the life's thread
of one wave-thrasher; wedged in his throat
the iron dart; with difficulty then
did he swim through the deep, until death took him.
They struck him as he swam, and straightaway,
with their boar-spears barbed and tanged;
gaffed and battered, he was brought to the cliff-top,
strange lurker of the waves. They looked with wonder
1440 at their grisly guest!

The Geat put on

the armour of a hero, unanxious for his life:
the manufacture of the mailed shirt,
figured and vast, that must venture in the deep,
made it such a bulwark to his bone-framed chest
that the savage attack of an incensed enemy
could do no harm to the heart within it.
His head was encircled by a silver helmet
that was to strike down through the swirl of water,
disturb the depths. Adorned with treasure,
1450 clasped with royal bands, it was right as at first
when the weapon-smith had wonderfully made it,
so that no sword should afterward be able to cut through
the defending wild boars that faced about it.
Not least among these mighty aids
was the hilted sword that Hrothgar's spokesman,
Unferth, lent him in his hour of trial.
Hrunting was its name; unique and ancient,
its edge was iron, annealed in venom
and tempered in blood; in battle it never
1460 failed any hero whose hand took it up
at his setting out on a stern adventure
for the house of foes. This was not the first time
that it had to do heroic work.

It would seem that the strapping son of Edgelaf
had forgotten the speech he had spoken earlier,
eloquent with wine, for he offered the weapon now
to the better swordsman; himself he would not go
beneath the spume to display his valour
and risk his life; he lost his reputation there

1470 for nerve and action. With the other man
it was otherwise once he had armed himself for battle.

Beowulf spoke, son of Edgetheow:
'I am eager to begin, great son of Healfdene.
Remember well, then, my wise lord,
provider of gold, what we agreed once before,
that if in your service it should so happen
that I am sundered from life, that you would assume
   the place
of a father towards me when I was gone.
Now extend your protection to the troop of my
   companions,
1480 my young fellows, if the fight should take me;
convey also the gifts that you have granted to me,
beloved Hrothgar, to my lord Hygelac.
For on seeing this gold, the Geat chieftain,
Hrethel's son, will perceive from its value
that I had met with magnificent patronage
from a giver of jewels, and that I had joy of him.
Let Unferth have the blade that I inherited
– he is a widely-known man – this wave-patterned sword
of rare hardness. With Hrunting shall I
1490 achieve this deed – or death shall take me!'

After these words the Weather-Geat prince
dived into the Mere – he did not care
to wait for an answer – and the waves closed over
the daring man. It was a day's space almost
before he could glimpse ground at the bottom.

The grim and greedy guardian of the flood,
keeping her hungry hundred-season watch,
discovered at once that one from above,
a human, had sounded the home of the monsters.
1500 She felt for the man and fastened upon him
her terrible hooks; but no harm came thereby
to the hale body within – the harness so ringed him
that she could not drive her dire fingers
through the mesh of the mail-shirt masking his limbs.

When she came to the bottom she bore him to her lair,
the mere-wolf, pinioning the mail-clad prince.
Not all his courage could enable him
to draw his sword; but swarming through the water,
throngs of sea-beasts threw themselves upon him
1510 with ripping tusks to tear his battle-coat,
tormenting monsters. Then the man found
that he was in some enemy hall
where there was no water to weigh upon him
and the power of the flood could not pluck him away,
sheltered by its roof: a shining light he saw,
a bright fire blazing clearly.

It was then that he saw the size of this water-hag,
damned thing of the deep. He dashed out his weapon,
not stinting the stroke, and with such strength and
        violence
1520 that the circled sword screamed on her head
a strident battle-song. But the stranger saw
his battle-flame refuse to bite
or hurt her at all; the edge failed
its lord in his need. It had lived through many

hand-to-hand conflicts, and carved through the helmets
of fated men. This was the first time
that this rare treasure had betrayed its name.
Determined still, intent on fame,
the nephew of Hygelac renewed his courage.

1530 Furious, the warrior flung it to the ground,
spiral-patterned, precious in its clasps,
stiff and steel-edged; his own strength would suffice him,
the might of his hands. A man must act so
when he means in a fight to frame himself
a long-lasting glory; it is not life he thinks of.

The Geat prince went for Grendel's mother,
seized her by the shoulder – he was not sorry to be
      fighting –
his mortal foe, and with mounting anger
the man hard in battle hurled her to the ground.

1540 She promptly repaid this present of his
as her ruthless hands reached out for him;
and the strongest of fighting-men stumbled in his
      weariness,
the firmest of foot-warriors fell to the earth.
She was down on this guest of hers and had drawn her
      knife,
broad, burnished of edge; for her boy was to be avenged,
her only son. Overspreading his back,
the shirt of mail shielded his life then,
barred the entry to edge and point.
Edgetheow's son would have ended his venture

1550 deep under ground there, the Geat fighter,
had not the battle-shirt then brought him aid,
his war-shirt of steel. And the wise Lord,

the holy God, gave out the victory;
the Ruler of the Heavens rightly settled it
as soon as the Geat regained his feet.

He saw among the armour there the sword to bring him
   victory,
a Giant-sword from former days: formidable were its edges,
a warrior's admiration. This wonder of its kind
was yet so enormous that no other man
1560 would be equal to bearing it in battle-play
 – it was a Giant's forge that had fashioned it so well.
The Scylding champion, shaking with war-rage,
caught it by its rich hilt, and, careless of his life,
brandished its circles, and brought it down in fury
to take her full and fairly across the neck,
breaking the bones; the blade sheared
through the death-doomed flesh. She fell to the ground;
the sword was gory; he was glad at the deed.

Light glowed out and illumined the chamber
1570 with a clearness such as the candle of heaven
sheds in the sky. He scoured the dwelling
in single-minded anger, the servant of Hygelac;
with his weapon high, and, holding to it firmly,
he stalked by the wall. Nor was the steel useless yet
to that man of battle, for he meant soon enough
to settle with Grendel for those stealthy raids
– there had been many of them – he had made on the
   West-Danes;
far more often than on that first occasion
when he had killed Hrothgar's hearth-companions,
1580 slew them as they slept, and in their sleep ate up

of the folk of Denmark fifteen good men,
carrying off another of them
in foul robbery. The fierce champion
now settled this up with him: he saw where Grendel
lay at rest, limp from the fight;
his life had wasted through the wound he had got
in the battle at Heorot. The body gaped open
as it now suffered the stroke after death
from the hard-swung sword; he had severed the neck.

1590 And above, the wise men who watched with Hrothgar
the depths of the pool descried soon enough
blood rising in the broken water
and marbling the surface. Seasoned warriors,
grey-headed, experienced, they spoke together,
said it seemed unlikely that they would see once more
the prince returning triumphant to seek out
their famous master. Many were persuaded
the she-wolf of the deep had done away with him.
The ninth hour had come; the keen-hearted Scyldings
1600 abandoned the cliff-head; the kindly gold-giver
turned his face homeward. But the foreigners sat on,
staring at the pool with sickness at heart,
hoping they would look again on their beloved captain,
believing they would not.
                                        The blood it had shed
made the sword dwindle into deadly icicles;
the war-tool wasted away. It was wonderful indeed
how it melted away entirely, as the ice does in the spring
when the Father unfastens the frost's grip,
unwinds the water's ropes – He who watches over
1610 the times and the seasons; He is the true God.

The Geat champion did not choose to take
any treasures from that hall, from the heaps he saw
      there,
other than that richly ornamented hilt,
and the head of Grendel. The engraved blade
had melted and burnt away: the blood was too hot,
the fiend that had died there too deadly by far.
The survivor of his enemies' onslaught in battle
now set to swimming, and struck up through the water;
both the deep reaches and the rough wave-swirl
1620 were thoroughly cleansed, now the creature from the
      otherworld
drew breath no longer in this brief world's space.

Then the seamen's Helm came swimming up
strongly to land, delighting in his sea-trove,
those mighty burdens that he bore along with him.
They went to meet him, a manly company,
thanking God, glad of their lord,
seeing him safe and sound once more.
Quickly the champion's corselet and helmet
were loosened from him. The lake's waters,
1630 sullied with blood, slept beneath the sky.

Then they turned away from there and retraced their
      steps,
pacing the familiar paths back again
as bold as kings, carefree at heart.
The carrying of the head from the cliff by the Mere
was no easy task for any of them,
brave as they were. They bore it up,
four of them, on a spear, and transported back

Grendel's head to the gold-giving hall.
Warrior-like they went, and it was not long
1640 before they came, the fourteen bold Geats,
marching to the hall, and, among the company
walking across the land, their lord the tallest.
The earl of those thanes then entered boldly
– a man who had dared deeds and was adorned with their
      glory,
a man of prowess – to present himself to Hrothgar.
Then was the head of Grendel, held up by its locks,
manhandled in where men were drinking;
it was an ugly thing for the earls and their queen,
an awesome sight; they eyed it well.

1650 Beowulf spoke, son of Edgetheow:
'Behold! What you see here, O son of Healfdene,
prince of the Scyldings, was pleasant freight for us:
– these trophies from the lake betoken victory!

   Not easily did I survive
the fight under water; I performed this deed
not without a struggle. Our strife had ended
at its very beginning if God had not saved me.
Nothing could I perform in that fight with Hrunting,
it had no effect, fine weapon though it be.
1660 But the Guide of mankind granted me the sight
– He often brings aid to the friendless –
of a huge Giant-sword hanging on the wall,
ancient and shining – and I snatched up the weapon.
When the hour afforded, in that fight I slew
the keepers of the hall. The coiling-patterned
blade burnt all away, as the blood sprang forth,

the hottest ever shed; the hilt I took from them.
So I avenged the violent slaughter
and outrages against the Danes; indeed it was fitting.
1670 Now, I say, you may sleep in Heorot
free from care – your company of warriors
and every man of your entire people,
both the young men and the guard. Gone is the need
to fear those fell attacks of former times
on the lives of your earls, my lord of the Scyldings.'

Then the golden hilt was given into the hand
of the older warrior, the white-haired leader.
A Giant had forged it. With the fall of the demons
it passed into the possession of the prince of the Danes,
1680 this work of wonder-smiths. The world was rid
of that invidious enemy of God
and his mother also, with their murders upon them;
and the hilt now belonged to the best of the kings
who ruled the earth in all the North
and distributed treasure between the seas.
Hrothgar looked on that long-treasured hilt
before he spoke. The spring was cut on it
of the primal strife, with the destruction at last
of the race of Giants by the rushing Flood,
1690 a terrible end. Estranged was that race
from the Lord of Eternity: the tide of water
was the final reward that the Ruler sent them.
On clear gold labels let into the cross-piece
it was rightly told in runic letters,
set down and sealed, for whose sake it was
that the sword was first forged, that finest of iron,
spiral-hilted, serpent-bladed.

At the speaking of the wise
son of Healfdene the hall was silent:
'One who has tendered justice and truth to his people,
1700 their shepherd from of old, surely may say this,
remembering all that's gone – that this man was born
to be the best of men. Beowulf, my friend,
your name shall resound in the nations of the earth
that are furthest away.

How wise you are to bear
your great strength so peaceably! I shall perform my
        vows
agreed in our forewords. It is granted to your people
that you shall live to be a long-standing comfort
and bulwark to the heroes.

Heremod was not so
for the honoured Scyldings, the sons of Edgewela:
1710 his manhood brought not pleasure but a plague upon us,
death and destruction to the Danish tribes.
In his fits he would cut down his comrade in war
and his table-companion – until he turned away
from the feastings of men, that famous prince.
This though the Almighty had exalted him in the bliss
of strength and vigour, advancing him far
above all other men. Yet inwardly his heart-hoard
grew raw and blood-thirsty; no rings did he give
to the Danes for his honour. And he dwelt an outcast,
1720 paid the penalty for his persecution of them
by a life of sorrow. Learn from this, Beowulf:
study openhandedness! It is for your ears that I relate
        this,
and I am old in winters.

                         It is wonderful to recount
how in his magnanimity the Almighty God
deals out wisdom, dominion and lordship
among mankind. The Master of all things
will sometimes allow to the soul of a man
of well-known kindred to wander in delight:
He will grant him earth's bliss in his own homeland,
1730 the sway of the fortress-city of his people,
and will give him to rule regions of the world,
wide kingdoms: he cannot imagine,
in his unwisdom, that an end will come.
His life of bounty is not blighted by hint
of age or ailment; no evil care
darkens his mind, malice nowhere
bares the sword-edge, but sweetly the world
swings to his will; worse is not looked for.
At last his part of pride within him
1740 waxes and climbs, the watchman of the soul
slumbering the while. That sleep is too deep,
tangled in its cares! Too close is the slayer
who shoots the wicked shaft from his bow!
For all his armour he is unable to protect himself:
the insidious bolt buries in his chest,
the crooked counsels of the accursed one.
What he has so long enjoyed he rejects as too little;
in niggardly anger renounces his lordly
gifts of gilt torques, forgets and misprises
1750 his fore-ordained part, endowed thus by God,
the Master of Glory, with these great bounties.
And ultimately the end must come,
the frail house of flesh must crumble
and fall at its hour. Another then takes

the earl's inheritance; open-handedly
he gives out its treasure, regardless of fear.

Beloved Beowulf, best of warriors,
resist this deadly taint, take what is better,
your lasting profit. Put away arrogance,
1760 noble fighter! The noon of your strength
shall last for a while now, but in a little time
sickness or a sword will strip it from you:
either enfolding flame or a flood's billow
or a knife-stab or the stoop of a spear
or the ugliness of age; or your eyes' brightness
lessens and grows dim. Death shall soon
have beaten you then, O brave warrior!

So it is with myself. I swayed the Ring-Danes
for fifty years here, defending them in war
1770 with ash and with edge over the earth's breadth
against many nations; until I numbered at last
not a single adversary beneath the skies' expanse.
But what change of fortune befell me at my hearth
with the coming of Grendel; grief sprang from joy
when the old enemy entered our hall!
Great was the pain that persecution
thrust upon me. Thanks be to God,
the Lord everlasting, that I have lived until this day,
seen out this age of ancient strife
1780 and set my gaze upon this gory head!
But join those who are seated, and rejoice in the feast,
O man clad in victory! We shall divide between us
many treasures when morning comes.'

The Geat went most gladly to take
his seat at the bench, at the bidding of the wise one.
Quite as before, the famous men,
guests of the hall, were handsomely feasted
on this new occasion. Then night's darkness
grew on the company. The guard arose,
1790 for their wise leader wished to rest,
the grey-haired Scylding. The Geat was ready enough
to go to his bed too, brave shieldsman.

The bower-thane soon brought on his way
this fight-wearied and far-born man.
His courteous office was to care for all
a guest's necessities, such as at that day
the wants of a seafaring warrior might be.
The hero took his rest; the hall towered up
gilded, wide-gabled, its guest within sleeping
1800 until the black raven blithe-hearted greeted
the heaven's gladness. Hastening, the sunlight
shook out above the shadows. Sharp were the bold ones,
each atheling eager to set off,
back to his homeland: the high-mettled stranger
wished to be forging far in his ship.
That hardy man ordered Hrunting to be carried
back to the son of Edgelaf, bade him accept again
his well-loved sword; said that he accounted it
formidable in the fight, a good friend in war,
1810 thanked him for the loan of it, without the least finding fault
with the edge of that blade; ample was his spirit!

By then the fighting-men were fairly armed-up
and ready for the journey; the Joy of the Danes went,

a prince, to the high seat where Hrothgar was,
one hero brave in battle hailed the other.

Beowulf then spoke, son of Edgetheow.
'We now wish to say, seafarers who
are come from far, how keenly we desire
to return again to Hygelac. Here we were rightly,
1820 royally, treated; you have entertained us well.
If I can ever on this earth earn of you,
O lord of men, more of your love
than I have so far done, by deeds of war,
I shall at once be ready. If ever I hear
that the neighbouring tribes intend your harm,
as those who hate you have done in the past,
I'll bring a thousand thanes and heroes
here to help you. As for Hygelac, I know
that the Lord of the Geats, Guide of his flock,
1830 young though he is, will yield his support
both in words and deeds so I may do you honour
and bring you a grove of grey-tipped spears
and my strength in aid when you are short of men.
Further, when Hrethric shall have it in mind
to come, as a king's son, to the courts of the Geats
he shall find many friends there. Far countries are seen
by a man of mark to much advantage.'

Hrothgar spoke to him in answer:
'These words you have delivered, the Lord in His wisdom
1840 put in your heart. I have heard no man
of the age that you are utter such wisdom.
You are rich in strength and ripe of mind,
you are wise in your utterance. If ever it should happen

that spear or other spike of battle,
sword or sickness, should sweep away
the son of Hrethel, your sovereign lord,
shepherd of his people, my opinion is clear,
that the Sea-Geats will not be seeking for a better
man to be their king and keep their war-hoard,
1850 if you still have life and would like to rule
the kingdom of your kinsmen. As I come to know
your temper, dear Beowulf, the better it pleases me.
You have brought it about that both the peoples,
the Sea-Geats and the Spear-Danes,
shall share out peace; the shock of war,
the old sourness, shall cease between us.
So long as I shall rule the reaches of this kingdom
we shall exchange wealth; a chief shall greet
his fellow with gifts over the gannet's bath
1860 as the ship with curved prow crosses the seas
with presents and pledges. Your people, I know,
always open-natured in the old manner,
are fast to friends and firm toward enemies.'

Then the Shield of the Heroes, Healfdene's son,
presented him with twelve new treasures in the hall,
bade him with these tokens betake himself
safe to his people; and soon return again.
Then that king of noble race, ruler of the Scyldings,
embraced and kissed that best of thanes,
1870 taking him by the neck; tears fell from
the grey-haired one. With the wisdom of age
he foresaw two things, the second more likely,
that they would never again greet one another,
meet thus as heroes. The man was so dear to him

that he could not stop the surging in his breast;
but hidden in the heart, held fast in its strings,
a deep longing for this dearly loved man
burned against the blood.

                    Beowulf went from him,
trod the green earth, a gold-resplendent warrior
1880 rejoicing in his rings. Riding at anchor
the strayer of ocean stayed for her master.
Chiefly the talk returned as they walked
to Hrothgar's giving. He was a king
blameless in all things, until old age at last,
that brings down so many, removed his proud strength.

They came then to the sea-flood, the spirited band
of warrior youth, wearing the ring-meshed
coat of mail. The coastguard saw
the heroes approaching, as he had done before.
1890 Nor was it ungraciously that he greeted the strangers
from his ridge by the cliff; but rode down to meet them:
how welcome they would be to the Weather-Geats, he said
to those shipward-bound men in their shining armour.
The wide sea-boat with its soaring prow
was loaded at the beach there with battle-raiment,
with horses and arms. High rose the mast
above the lord Hrothgar's hoard of gifts.
To the boat-guard Beowulf gave
a gold-cleated sword; it gained the man
1900 much honour on the mead-benches,
that treasured heirloom. Out moved the boat then
to divide the deep water, left Denmark behind.
A special sea-dress, a sail, was hoisted
and belayed to the mast. The beams spoke.

The wind did not hinder the wave-skimming ship
as it ran through the seas, but the sea-going craft
with foam at its throat, furled back the waves,
her ring-bound prow planing the waters
till they caught sight of the cliffs of the Geats
1910 and headlands they knew. The hull drove ahead,
urged by the breeze, and beached on the shore.

The harbour-guard was waiting at the water's edge;
his eye had been scouring the stretches of the flood
in a long look-out for these loved men.
Now he moored the broad-ribbed boat in the sand,
held fast with hawsers, so no heft of the waves
should drive away again those darling timbers.
He had the heroes' hoard brought ashore,
their gold-plated armour. To go to their lord
1920 was now but a step, to see again Hygelac
the son of Hrethel, at his home where he dwells
himself with his hero-band, hard by the sea-wall.

That was a handsome hall there. And high within it sat
a king of great courage. His consort was young,
but wise and discreet for one who had lived
so few years at court; the queen's name was *Hygd*,
Hareth's daughter. When she dealt out treasure
to the Geat nation, the gifts were generous,
there was nothing narrowly done.

                               It was not so with Modthryth,
1930 imperious queen, cruel to her people.
There was no one so rash among the retainers of the house
as to risk a look at her – except her lord himself –
turn his eyes on her, even by day;

or fatal bonds were fettled for him,
twisted by hand: and when hands had been laid on him
he could be sure that the sword would be present,
and settle it quickly, its spreading inlays
proclaim its killing-power. Unqueenly ways
for a woman to follow, that one who weaves peace,
1940 though of matchless looks, should demand the life
of a well-loved man for an imagined wrong!
Hemming's son *Offa* put an end to that.
And the ale-drinkers then told a tale quite different:
little was the hurt or harm that she brought
on her subjects then, as soon as she was given,
gold-decked, in marriage, to the mighty young champion
of valiant lineage, when she voyaged out
on the pale flood at her father's bidding
to the hall of Offa. All that followed
1950 of a life destined to adorn a throne
she employed well, and was well-loved for it,
strong in her love for that leader of heroes,
the outstanding man, as I have heard tell,
of all mankind's mighty race
from sea to sea. So it was that Offa,
brave with the spear, was spoken of abroad
for his wars and his gifts; he governed with wisdom
the land of his birth. To him was born Eomer,
helper of the heroes, Hemming's kinsman,
1960 Garmund's grandson, great in combat.

The war-man himself came walking along
by the broad foreshores with his band of picked men,
trod the sea-beach. From the south blazed

the sun, the world's candle. They carried themselves
     forward,
stepping on eagerly to the stronghold where
Ongentheow's conqueror, the earls' defender,
the warlike young king, was well-known for his
giving of neck-rings. The news of Beowulf's
return was rapidly told to Hygelac
1970 — that the shield of warriors, his own shoulder-companion,
had walked alive within the gates,
unscathed from the combat, and was coming to the hall.
The floor was quickly cleared of men
for the incoming guests, by order of the king.

When he had offered greetings in grave words,
as usage obliged him, to his lord of men,
the survivor of the fight sat facing the king,
kinsman and kinsman. Carrying the mead-cup
about the hall was Hareth's daughter,
1980 lover of the people, presenting the wine-bowl
to the hand of each Geat. Hygelac then made
of his near companion in that noble hall
courteous inquiry. Curiosity burned in him
to hear the adventures of this voyage of the Geats.

'What luck did you meet with, beloved Beowulf,
on your suddenly resolved seeking out
of distant strife over salt water,
battle at Heorot? Did you bring to that famous
leader Hrothgar some alleviation
1990 of those woes so widely known? Overwhelming doubts
troubled my mind, mistrusting this voyage
of my dear liegeman. Long did I beg you

never to meet with this murderous creature
but to let the South Danes themselves bring an end
to their feud with Grendel. God be thanked
that safe and sound I see you here today!'

Thus spoke Beowulf, son of Edgetheow:
'It has been told aloud, my lord Hygelac,
and to many men by now, the meeting that there was
2000   between myself and Grendel, the great time
we fought in that place where he had inflicted so much
grief and outrage, age-long disgrace
on the Victor-Scyldings. I avenged all.
No kinsman of Grendel shall have cause to take pride
in the sound that arose in the stretches of the night
— not the last of that alien and evil brood
on the face of the earth.
                 First I went in
to greet Hrothgar in the hall of the ring-giving.
As soon as the glorious son of Healfdene
2010   knew my mind, he immediately
offered me a seat at his sons' bench.
What hall-joys were there! A happier company
seated over mead I've not met with in my time
beneath the heavens. A noble princess
fit to be the pledge of peace between nations
would move through the young men in the hall,
stirring their spirits; bestowing a torque
often upon a warrior before she went to her seat.
Or the heroes would look on as Hrothgar's daughter
2020   bore the ale-flagon to each earl in turn.
I heard those who sat in the hall calling her

by the name of *Freawaru* as she fetched each warrior
the nailed treasure-cup.
                        She is betrothed to *Ingeld*,
this girl attired in gold, to the gracious son of Froda.
The Protector of the Danes has determined this
and accounts it wisdom, the keeper of the land,
thus to end all the feud and their fatal wars
by means of the lady. Yet when a lord is dead
it is seldom the slaying-spear sleeps for long –
2030   seldom indeed – dear though the bride may be.

    The lord of the Heathobards may not like it well
at the bringing home of his bride to the hall:
nor may it please every earl in that nation
to have the pride and daring of Denmark at table
– their guests resplendent in the spoil of their ancestors!
Heathobards had treasured these trenchant, ring-patterned
weapons until they could wield them no longer,
having taken part in that play of the shields
where they lost their lives and the lives of their friends.

2040   An old spear-fighter shall speak at the feast,
eyeing the hilt-ring – his heart grows fierce
as he remembers all the slaying of the men by the spear.
In his dark mood he deliberately
tries out the mettle of a man who is younger,
awakens his war-taste in words such as these:
"My friend, is that not a familiar sword?
Your father carried it forth to battle,
– excellent metal – masked as for war
on his last expedition. There the Danes slew him,
2050   the keen Scyldings, and kept the field

73

when Withergyld was dead, when the warriors had fallen.
The son of one of his slayers now
sports the weapon here, and, spurning our hall-floor,
boasts of the killing: he carries at his side
the prize that you should possess by right."

    With such biting words of rebuke and reminder
he taunts him at every turn; until the time comes
when one sleeps blood-stained from the blow of a sword:
the follower of the lady forfeits with his life
2060 for the actions of his father; the other contrives
to lose himself, and lives; the land is familiar to him.
Both sides then will break the pact
sworn by the earls; and Ingeld's vengefulness
will well up in him, overwhelming gall
shall cause his wife-love to cool thereafter.
So I do not believe that this liking of the Heathobards
for alliance with the Danes is all what it seems,
or that their friendship is sound.
                       I shall speak further
of Grendel again, O giver of treasure,
2070 that you may rightly know the result of the champions'
hand-to-hand meeting. When heaven's jewel
had glided from the world, the wrathful creature,
dire dusk-fiend, came down to seek us out
where, still whole, we held the building.
The weight of the fight fell on Handscio,
the doomed blow came down on him; he died the first,
a warrior in his harness; the hero, my fellow,
was ground to death between Grendel's jaws,
our friend's body was bolted down whole.
2080 But the bloody-toothed slayer, bent on destruction,

was not going to go from that gold-giving hall
any the sooner: not empty-handed!
Proud of his might, he made proof of me,
groped out his greedy palm. A glove hung from it,
uncouth and huge, clasped strangely,
and curiously contrived; it was cobbled together
all of dragons' skins, and with devilish skill.
It was inside this bag that the bold marauder
was going to put me, guiltless as I was,
2090   as the first of his catch; but he could not manage it
once I had stood up in anger against him.
Too long to repeat here how I paid back
the enemy of the people for his every crime;
but to your people, O my prince, my performance there
will bring honour. He broke away,
tasted life's joys for a little while,
but his strong right hand stayed behind
in the hall of Heorot; humbled he went thence
and sank despairing in the depths of the Mere.

2100   For this deadly fight the Friend of the Scyldings
recompensed me with plated gold,
a mort of treasure, when the morrow came
and we had benched ourselves at the banqueting table.
There was music and laughter, lays were sung:
the veteran of the Scyldings, versed in saga,
would himself fetch back far-off times to us;
the daring-in-battle would address the harp,
the joy-wood, delighting; or deliver a reckoning
both true and sad; or he would tell us the story
2110 of some wonderful adventure, valiant-hearted king.
Or the seasoned warrior, wrapped in age,

would again fall to fabling of his youth
and the days of his battle-strength; his breast was troubled
as his mind filled with the memories of those years.

And thus we spent the space of a day there
seeking delight, until the ensuing dusk
came to mankind. Quick on its heels
the mother of Grendel moved to her revenge,
spurred on by sorrow; her son was death-taken
2120 by Geat warspite. That gruesome she
avenged her son, struck down a warrior,
and boldly enough! The breath was taken
from the ancient counsellor, Ashhere, there.
Nor could the Danish people, when day came,
give their death-wearied dear one to be burned,
escort him to the pyre: she had carried the body
to the mountain-torrent's depth in her monstrous embrace.
This was for Hrothgar the harshest of the blows
that since so long had fallen on the leader of the people.
2130 Distraught with care, the king then asked of me
a noble action – and in your name, Hygelac –
that I should risk my life among the rush of waters
and perform a great deed; he promised me reward.

Far and wide it is told how I found in the surges
the grim and terrible guardian of the deep.
After a hard hand-to-hand struggle
the whirlpool boiled with the blood of the mother;
I had hewn off her head in that hall underground
with a sword of huge size. I survived that fight
2140 not without difficulty; but my doom was not yet.

The protector of warriors rewarded me
with a heap of treasure, Healfdene's son.
The ways of that king accorded to usage:
I was not to forgo the guerdon he had offered,
the meed of my strength; he bestowed upon me
the treasures I would have desired, the son of Healfdene;
now, brave king, I bring them to you.
I rejoice to present them. Joy, for me, always
lies in your gift. Little family
2150 do I have in the world, Hygelac, besides yourself.'

Then he bade them bring in the boar's head standard,
the battle-dwarfing helmet, the hoar war-shirt
and the lambent sword; and delivered this speech:
'Hrothgar gave me all this garb of war
with one word – the wisest of princes –
that I should first relate to you whose legacy it is.
His brother Heorogar had it, he told me,
for a long while, as Lord of the Scyldings,
yet chose not to give this guardian of his breast
2160 to his own son, the spirited Heoroweard,
friend though he was to him.
                              Flourish in the use of it!'

I heard that four fast-stepping horses
followed these treasures, a team of bays,
matching as apples. All these he gave him,
both horses and armour – the act of a kinsman!
A kinsman knits no nets of malice
darkly for his fellow. Does he devise the end
of the man that is next to him? The nephew of Hygelac

held fast to that man hardy in battle;
2170 each thought only of the other's welfare.

Beowulf, I heard, gave Hygd the neck-ring,
the wonderful treasure work Wealhtheow had given him
– high was her breeding – and three horses also,
graceful in their gait, and with gay saddles.
Her breast was made more beautiful by the jewel.

Such was the showing of the son of Edgetheow,
known for his combats and his courage in action.
His dealings were honourable: in drink he did not strike
at the slaves of his hearth; his heart was not savage.
2180 The hero guarded well the great endowment
God had bestowed on him, a strength unequalled
among mankind. He had been misprised for long,
the sons of the Geats seeing little in him
and the lord of the Weather-Geats not willing to pay
            him
much in the way of honour on the mead-benches.
They firmly believed in his laziness
– 'the atheling was idle'! But for all such humblings
time brought reversal, invested him with glory.

Then the king bold in war, keeper of the warriors,
2190 required them to bring in the bequest of Hrethel,
elaborate in gold; the Geats at that day
had no more royal treasure of the rank of sword.
This he then laid in the lap of Beowulf
and bestowed on him an estate of seven thousand hides,
a chief's stool and a hall. Inherited land,
a domain by birthright, had come down to them both

in the Geat nation; the greater region
to the better-born of them – the broad kingdom.

But it fell out after, in other days,
among the hurl of battle – when Hygelac lay dead
and the bills of battle had dealt death to his Heardred,
despite the shield's shelter, when the Scylfings found him
amid his conquering people, and those keen war-wolves
grimly hemmed in Hereric's nephew –
that the broad kingdom came by this turn
into Beowulf's hands.

                Half a century
he ruled it, well: until One began
– the king had grown grey in the guardianship of the land –
to put forth his power in the pitch-black night-times
– the hoard-guarding *Dragon* of a high barrow
raised above the moor.

                   Men did not know
of the way underground to it; but one man did enter,
went right inside, reached the treasure,
the heathen hoard, and his hand fell
on a golden goblet. The guardian, however,
if he had been caught sleeping by the cunning of the thief,
did not conceal this loss. It was not long till the near-
dwelling people discovered that the dragon was angry.

The causer of his pain had not purposed this;
it was without relish that he had robbed the hoard;
necessity drove him. The nameless slave
of one of the warriors, wanting shelter,
on the run from a flogging, had felt his way inside,
a sin-tormented soul. When he saw what was there

the intruder was seized with sudden terror;
but for all his fear, the unfortunate wretch
still took the golden treasure-cup . . .
There were heaps of hoard-things in this hall underground
which once in gone days gleamed and rang;
2230   the treasure of a race rusting derelict.

In another age an unknown man,
brows bent, had brought and hid here
the beloved hoard. The whole race
death-rapt, and of the ring of earls
one left alive; living on in that place
heavy with friend-loss, the hoard-guard
waited the same weird. His wit acknowledged
that the treasures gathered and guarded over the years
were his for the briefest while.
                  The barrow stood ready
2240   on flat ground where breakers beat at the headland,
new, near at hand, made narrow of access.
The keeper of rings carried into it
the earls' holdings, the hoard-worthy part
fraught with gold, and few words he spoke:
'Hold, ground, the gold of the earls!
Men could not. Cowards they were not
who took it from thee once, but war-death took them,
that stops life, struck them, spared not one
man of my people, passed on now.
2250   They have had their hall-joys. I have not with me
a man able to unsheathe this . . .
Who shall polish this plated vessel,
this treasured cup? The company is elsewhere.

This hardened helmet healed with gold
shall lose its shell. They sleep now
whose work was to burnish the battle-masks;
so with the cuirass that in the crash took
bite of iron among breaking shields:
it moulders with the man. This mail-shirt travelled far,
2260   hung from a shoulder that shouldered warriors:
it shall not jingle again.

               There's no joy from harp-play,
glee-wood's gladness, no good hawk
swings through hall now, no swift horse
tramps at the threshold. Terrible slaughter
has carried into darkness many kindreds of mankind.'

So the sole survivor, in sorrowful mood,
bewailed his grief; he wandered cheerless
through days and nights until death's flood
reached to his heart.

             The Ravager of the night,
2270   the burner who has sought out barrows from of old,
then found this hoard of undefended joy.
The smooth evil dragon swims through the gloom
enfolded in flame; the folk of that country
hold him in dread. He is doomed to seek out
hoards in the ground, and guard for an age there
the heathen gold: much good does it do him!

Thus for three hundred winters this waster of peoples
guarded underground the great hoard-hall
with his enormous might; until a man awoke
2280   the anger in his breast by bearing to his master
the plated goblet as a peace-offering,

a token of new fealty. Thus the treasure was lightened
and the treasure-house was breached; the boon was
      granted
to the luckless slave, and his lord beheld
for the first time that work of a former race of men.

The waking of the worm awoke a new feud:
he glided along the rock, glared at the sight
of a foeman's footprint: far too near his head
the intruder had stepped as he stole by him!
2290 (An undoomed man may endure affliction
and even exile lightly, for as long as the Ruler
continues to protect him.) The treasure-guard eagerly
quartered the ground to discover the man
who had done him wrong during his sleep.
Seething with rage, he circled the barrow's
whole outer wall, but no hint of a man
showed in the wilderness. Yet war's prospect pleased him,
the thought of battle-action! He went back into the
      mound
to search for the goblet, and soon saw that one
2300 of the tribe of men had tampered with the gold
of the glorious hoard.
                    The hoard's guardian
waited until evening only with difficulty.
The barrow-keeper was bursting with rage:
his fire would cruelly requite the loss
of the dear drinking-vessel.
                    At last day was gone,
to the worm's delight; he delayed no further
inside his walls, but issued forth flaming,
armed with fire.

That was a fearful beginning
for the people of that country; uncomfortable and swift
2310 was the end to be likewise for their lord and treasure-giver!

So the visitant began to vomit flames
and burn the bright dwellings; the blazing rose skyward
and men were afraid: the flying scourge
did not mean to leave one living thing.
On every side the serpent's ravages,
the spite of the foe, sprang to the eye –
how this hostile assailant hated and injured
the men of the Geats. Before morning's light
he flew back to the hoard in its hidden chamber.
2320 He had poured out fire and flame on the people,
he had put them to the torch; he trusted now to the
          barrow's walls
and to his fighting strength. His faith misled him.

Beowulf was acquainted quickly enough
with the truth of the horror, for his own hall had itself
been swallowed in flame, the finest of buildings,
and the gift-stool of the Geats. Grief then struck
into his ample heart with anguished keenness.
The chieftain supposed he had sorely angered
the Ruler of all, the eternal Lord,
2330 by breach of ancient law. His breast was thronged
with dark unaccustomed care-filled thoughts.
The fiery dragon's flames had blasted
all the land by the sea, and its safe stronghold,
the fortress of the people. The formidable king
of the Geats now planned to punish him for this.
The champion of the fighting-men, chief of the earls,

gave orders for the making of a marvellous shield
worked all in iron; well he knew
that a linden shield would be of little service
2340 — wood against fire. For the foremost of athelings
the term of his days in this transitory world
was soon to be endured; it was the end, too, for the dragon's
long watch over the wealth of the hoard.

The distributor of rings disdained to go
with a troop of men or a mighty host
to seek the far-flier. He had no fear for himself
and discounted the worm's courage and strength,
its prowess in battle. Battles in plenty
he had survived; valiant in all dangers,
2350 he had come through many clashes since his cleansing
    of Heorot
and his extirpation of the tribe of Grendel,
hated race.
        That was hardly the least
of hand-to-hand combats when Hygelac was slain,
when that kindly lord of peoples, the king of the Geats,
the son of Hrethel, among the hurl of battle
slaked the sword's thirst on the soil of Friesland
and the blows beat down on him!
                    Beowulf came away
by the use of his force in a feat of swimming;
alone into the ocean he leapt, holding
2360 thirty men's mail-coats on his arm.

There was little cause for crowing among the Hetware
about their conduct of the foot-fight: they carried their
    lindens

forward against him; but few came back
from the wolf in war, walked home again.
Solitary and wretched was the son of Edgetheow
on the sweep of waters as he swam back to his people.
There Hygd offered him the hoard and the kingdom,
the gift-stool and its treasure; not trusting that her son
would be able to hold the inherited seats
2370 against foreign peoples now his father was dead.
But the bereaved people could arrive at no conditions
under which the atheling would accept the kingdom
or allow himself to be lord over Heardred.
Rather he fostered him among the people with friendly
       counsel,
with kindliness and respect, until he came of age
and ruled the Geats.
               Guests sought out Heardred,
outcasts from oversea: Ohthere's sons.

They had risen against Onela, ruler of the Scylfings,
highest of the princes who provided treasure
2380 in all the sea-coasts of the Swedish realms,
a famous lord. This led to the end
of Hygelac's son; his hospitality
cost him a weapon-thrust and a wound to the life.
Ongentheow's son, Onela, turned
to seek his home again once Heardred was dead;
the gift-stool and the ruling of the Geat people
he left to Beowulf; who was a brave king,
and kept it before his mind to requite his lord's death.
In after-days he was Eadgils' friend
2390 when Eadgils was deserted, supporting his cause
across the wide water with weapons and an army,

Ohthere's son; who took his own revenge
by terror-campaigns that at last trapped Onela.

So the son of Edgetheow survived unscathed
each of these combats, calamitous onslaughts,
works of prowess: until this one day
when he must wage war on the serpent.
The Lord of the Geats went with eleven companions
to set eyes on the dragon; his anger rose in him.

2400   He had by then discovered the cause of the attack
that had ravaged his people; the precious drinking-cup
had come into his hands from the hands of the informer.
He who had brought about the beginning of the feud
now made the thirteenth man in their company,
a miserable captive; cowed, he must show them
the way to the place, an unwilling guide.
For he alone knew the knoll and its earth-hall,
hard by the strand and the strife of the waves,
the underground hollow heaped to the roof
2410   with intricate treasures. Attendant on the gold
was that underground ancient, eager as a wolf,
an awesome guardian; it was no easy bargain
for any mortal man to make himself its owner.

The stern war-king sat on the headland,
spoke encouragement to the companions of his hearth,
the gold-friend of the Geats. Gloomy was his spirit though,
death-eager, wandering; the weird was at hand
that was to overcome the old man there,
seek his soul's hoard, and separate
2420   the life from the body; not for long now
would the atheling's life be lapped in flesh.

Beowulf spoke, son of Edgetheow:
'Many were the struggles I survived in youth
in times of danger; I do not forget them.
When that open-handed lord beloved by the people
received me from my father I was seven years old:
King Hrethel kept and fostered me,
gave me treasure and table-room, true to our kinship.
All his life he had as little hatred for me,
2430 a warrior in hall, as he had for a son,
Herebeald, or Hathkin, or Hygelac my own lord.

   A murderous bed was made for the eldest
by the act of a kinsman, contrary to right:
a shaft from Hathkin's horn-tipped bow
shot down the man that should have become his lord;
mistaking his aim, he struck his kinsman,
his own brother, with the blood-stained arrow-head.
A sin-fraught conflict that could not be settled,
unthinkable in the heart; yet thus it was,
2440 and the atheling lost his life unavenged.

   Grief such as this a grey-headed man
might feel if he saw his son in youth
riding the gallows. Let him raise the lament then,
a song of sorrow, while his son hangs there,
a sport for the raven. Remedy is there none
that an age-stricken man may afford him then.
Every morning reminds him again
that his son has gone elsewhere; another son,
an heir in his courts, he cares not to wait for,
2450 now that the first has found his deeds
have come to an end in the constriction of death.

He sorrows to see among his son's dwellings
the wasted wine-hall, the wind's home now,
bereft of all joy. The riders are sleeping,
the heroes in the grave. The harp does not sound,
there is no laughter in the yard as there used to be of old.
He goes then to his couch, keens the lament
for his one son alone there; too large now seem to him
his houses and fields.
                              The Helm of the Geats
2460 sustained a like sorrow for Herebeald
surging in his heart. Hardly could he settle
the feud by imposing a price on the slayer;
no more could he offer actions to that warrior
manifesting hatred; though he held him not dear.

     Hard did this affliction fall upon him:
he renounced men's cheer, chose God's light.
But he left to sons his land and stronghold
at his life's faring-forth – as the fortunate man does.

     On Hrethel's death the hatred and strife
2470 of the Swedes and the Geats, the grievances between them,
broke into bitter war across the broad water.
The sons of Ongentheow were strong fighters,
active in war; they would not keep
peace on the lakes, but plotted many
a treacherous ambush about Hreosnabeorgh.

     It has come to be known that my kinsmen and friends
revenged both the feud and the violent attack,
though the price that one of them paid was his life,
a hard bargain. That battle proved

2480   mortal for Hathkin, Master of the Geats.
      But came the morrow, and a kinsman, as I heard,
      avenged him on his slayer with the sword's edge:
      in his attack on Eofor, Ongentheow's
      war-mask shattered, and the Scylfing patriarch
      fell pale from the wound; the wielding hand
      forgot not the feud, flinched not from the death-blow.

     I had the fortune in that battle, by my bright sword,
      to make return to Hygelac for the treasures he had given
          me.
      He had granted me land, land to enjoy
2490   and leave to my heirs. Little need was there
      that Hygelac should go to the Gifthas or the Spear-Danes
      or seek out ever in the Swedish kingdom
      a weaker champion, and chaffer for his services.
      I was always before him in the footing host,
      by myself in the front.
              So, while I live,
      I shall always do battle, while this blade lasts
      that early and late has often served me
      since, with my bare hands, I broke Dayraven,
      the champion of the Franks, before the flower of the host.
2500   He was not to be permitted to present his Frisian lord
      with the breast-armour that had adorned Hygelac,
      for he was slain in the struggle, the standard-bearer,
      noble in his prowess. It was not my sword
      that broke his bone-cage and the beatings of his heart
      but my warlike hand-grasp.
                  Now shall hard edge,
    hand and blade, do battle for the hoard!'

Beowulf made speech, spoke a last time
a word of boasting: 'Battles in plenty
I ventured in youth; and I shall venture this feud
2510 and again achieve glory, the guardian of my people,
old though I am, if this evil destroyer
dares to come out of his earthen hall.'

Then he addressed each of the men there
on this last occasion, courageous helm-bearers,
cherished companions: 'I would choose not to take
any weapon to this worm, if I well knew
of some other fashion fitting to my boast
of grappling with this monster, as with Grendel before.
But as I must expect here the hot war-breath
2520 of venom and fire, for this reason I have
my board and corselet. From the keeper of the barrow
I shall not flee one foot; but further than that
shall be worked out at the wall as our weird is given us
by the Creator of men. My mood is strong;
I forgo further words against the winged fighter.

Men in armour! Your mail-shirts protect you:
await on the barrow the one of us two
who shall be better able to bear his wounds
after this onslaught. This affair is not for you,
2530 nor is it measured to any man but myself alone
to match strength with this monstrous being,
attempt this deed. By daring will I
win this gold; war otherwise
shall take your king, terrible life's-bane!'

The strong champion stood up beside his shield,
brave beneath helmet, he bore his mail-shirt
to the rocky cliff's foot, confident in his strength,
a single man; such is not the coward's way!
Then did the survivor of a score of conflicts,
2540 the battle-clashes of encountering armies,
excelling in manhood, see in the wall
a stone archway, and out of the barrow broke
a stream surging through it, a stream of fire
with waves of deadly flame; the dragon's breath
meant he could not venture into the vault near the
      hoard
for any time at all without being burnt.

Passion filled the prince of the Geats:
he allowed a cry to utter from his breast,
roared from his stout heart: as the horn clear in battle
2550 his voice re-echoed through the vault of grey stone.
The hoard-guard recognized a human voice,
and there was no more time for talk of friendship:
hatred stirred. Straightaway
the breath of the dragon billowed from the rock
in a hissing gust; the ground boomed.

He swung up his shield, overshadowed by the mound,
the lord of the Geats against this grisly stranger.
The temper of the twisted tangle-thing was fired
to close now in battle. The brave warrior-king
2560 shook out his sword so sharp of edge,
an ancient heirloom. Each of the pair,
intending destruction, felt terror at the other:
intransigent beside his towering shield

the lord of friends, while the fleetness of the serpent
wound itself together; he waited in his armour.
It came flowing forward, flaming and coiling,
rushing on its fate.

For the famous prince

the protection lent to his life and person
by the shield was shorter than he had shaped it to be.
2570 He must now dispute this space of time,
the first in his life when fate had not assigned him
the glory of the battle. The Geat chieftain
raised his hand, and reached down such a stroke
with his huge ancestral sword on the horribly-patterned
snake
that, meeting the bone, its bright edge turned
and it bit less strongly than its sorely-straitened lord
required of it then. The keeper of the barrow
after this stroke grew savage in mood,
spat death-fire; the sparks of their battle
2580 blazed into the distance.

He boasted of no triumphs then,

the gold-friend of the Geats, for his good old sword
bared in the battle, his blade, had failed him,
as such iron should not do.

That was no easy adventure,

when the celebrated son of Edgetheow
had to pass from that place on earth
and against his will take up his dwelling
in another place; as every man must give up
the days that are lent him.

It was not long again

to the next meeting of those merciless ones.
2590 The barrow-guard took heart: his breast heaved

with fresh out-breath: fire enclosed
the former folk-king; he felt bitter pain.

The band of picked companions did not come
to stand about him, as battle-usage asks
offspring of athelings; they escaped to the wood,
saved their lives.
             Sorrow filled
the breast of one man. The bonds of kinship
nothing may remove for a man who thinks rightly.
This was *Wiglaf*, Weoxstan's son,
2600 well-loved shieldsman, a Scylfing prince
of the stock of Alfhere; he could see his lord
tormented by the heat through his mask of battle.
He remembered then the favours he had formerly bestowed
       on him,
the wealthy dwelling-place of the Waymundings,
confirming him in the landrights his father had held.
He could not then hold back: hand gripped the yellow
linden-wood shield, shook out that ancient
sword that Eanmund, Ohthere's son,
had left among men.
            He met his end in battle,
2610 a friendless exile, felled by the sword
wielded by Weoxstan: who went back to his kinsmen
with the shining helm, the shirt of ring-mail
and the ancient giant-sword. All this war-harness,
eager for use, Onela then gave to him,
though it had been his nephew's; nor did he speak
of the blood-feud to the killer of his brother's son.
Weoxstan kept this war-gear many years,
sword and breast-armour, till his son was able

to perform manly deeds as his father had of old.
2620 He gave him among the Geats these garments of battle
of incalculable worth; then went his life's journey
wise and full of years.

For the youthful warrior
this was the first occasion when he was called on to stand
at his dear lord's shoulder in the shock of battle.
His courage did not crumble, nor did his kinsman's
 heirloom
weaken at the war-play: as the worm found
when they had got to grips with one another.

Wiglaf then spoke many words that were fitting,
addressed his companions; dark was his mood.
2630 'I remember the time, as we were taking mead
in the banqueting hall, when we bound ourselves
to the gracious lord who granted us arms,
that we would make return for these trappings of war,
these helms and hard swords, if an hour such as this
should ever chance for him. He chose us himself
out of all his host for this adventure here,
expecting action; he armed me with you
because he accounted us keen under helmet,
men able with the spear – even though our lord
2640 intended to take on this task of courage
as his own share, as shepherd of the people,
and champion of mankind in the achieving of glory
and deeds of daring.

That day has now come
when he stands in need of the strength of good fighters,
our lord and liege. Let us go to him,
help our leader for as long as it requires,

the fearsome fire-blast. I had far rather
that the flame should enfold my flesh-frame there
alongside my gold-giver – as God knows of me.
2650 To bear our shields back to our homes
would seem unfitting to me, unless first we have been able
to kill the foe and defend the life
of the prince of the Weather-Geats. I well know
that former deeds deserve not that, alone
of the flower of the Geats, he should feel the pain,
sink in the struggle; sword and helmet,
corselet and mail-shirt, shall be our common gear.'

He strode through the blood-smoke, bore his war-helmet
to the aid of his lord, uttered few words:
2660 'Beloved Beowulf, bear all things well!
You gave it out long ago in your youth
that, living, you would not allow your glory
ever to abate. Bold-tempered chieftain,
famed for your deeds, you must defend your life now
with all your strength. I shall help you.'

When these words had been spoken, the worm came on
        wrathful,
attacked a second time, terrible visitant,
sought out his foes in a surge of flame,
the hated men.
                Mail-shirt did not serve
2670 the young spear-man; and shield was withered
back to the boss by the billow of fire;
but when the blazing had burnt up his own,
the youngster stepped smartly to take
the cover of his kinsman's. Then did that kingly warrior

remember his deeds again and dealt out a sword-blow
with his full strength: it struck into the head
with annihilating weight. But Nailing snapped,
failed in the battle, Beowulf's sword
of ancient grey steel. It was not granted to him
2680 that an iron edge could ever lend him
help in a battle; his hand was too strong.
I have heard that any sword, however hardened by
            wounds,
that he bore into battle, his blow would overtax
– any weapon whatever; it was the worse for him.

A third time the terrible fire-drake
remembered the feud. The foe of the people
rushed in on the champion when a chance offered:
seething with warspite, he seized his whole neck
between bitter fangs: blood covered him,
2690 Beowulf's life-blood, let in streams.
Then I heard how the earl alongside the king
in the hour of need made known the valour,
boldness and strength that were bred in him.
His hand burned as he helped his kinsman,
but the brave soldier in his splendid armour
ignored the head and hit the attacker
somewhat below it, so that the sword went in,
flashing-hilted; and the fire began
to slacken in consequence.
                              The king once more
2700 took command of his wits, caught up a stabbing-knife
of the keenest battle-sharpness, that he carried in his
            harness:
and the Geats' Helm struck through the serpent's body.

So daring drove out life: they had downed their foe
by common action, the atheling pair,
and had made an end of him. So in the hour of need
a warrior must live! For the lord this was
the last victory in the list of his deeds
and works in the world. The wound that the earth-
       drake
had first succeeded in inflicting on him
2710 began to burn and swell; he swiftly felt
the bane beginning to boil in his chest,
the poison within him. The prince walked across
to the side of the barrow, considering deeply;
he sat down on a ledge, looked at the giant-work,
saw how the age-old earth-hall contained
stone arches anchored on pillars.
Then that excellent thane with his own hands washed
his battle-bloodied prince, bathed with water
the famous leader, his friend and lord,
2720 sated with fighting; he unfastened his helmet.

Beowulf spoke; he spoke through the pain
of his fatal wound. He well knew
that he had come to the end of his allotted days,
his earthly happiness; all the number
of his days had disappeared: death was very near.
'I would now wish to give my garments in battle
to my own son, if any such
after-inheritor, an heir of my body,
had been granted to me. I have guarded this people
2730 for half a century; not a single ruler
of all the nations neighbouring about
has dared to affront me with his friends in war,

or threaten terrors. What the times had in store for me
I awaited in my homeland; I held my own,
sought no secret feud, swore very rarely
a wrongful oath.

                In all of these things,
sick with my life's wound, I may still rejoice:
for when my life shall leave my body
the Ruler of Men may not charge me
2740 with the slaughter of kinsmen.

                          Quickly go now,
beloved Wiglaf, and look upon the hoard
under the grey stone, now the serpent lies dead,
sleeps rawly wounded, bereft of his treasure.
Make haste, that I may gaze upon that golden inheritance,
that ancient wealth; that my eyes may behold
the clear skilful jewels: more calmly then may I
on the treasure's account take my departure
of life and of the lordship I have long held.'

Straightaway, as I have heard, the son of Weoxstan
2750 obeyed his wounded lord, weak from the struggle.
Following these words, he went in his ring-coat,
his broidered battle-tunic, under the barrow's roof.
Traversing the ledge to the treasure-house of jewels,
the brave young thane was thrilled by the sight
of the gold gleaming on the ground where it lay,
the devices by the wall and the den of the serpent,
winger of the darkness. Drinking-cups stood there,
the unburnished vessels of a vanished race,
their ornaments awry. Old and tarnished
2760 were the rows of helmets and the heaps of arm-rings,
twisted with cunning. Treasure can easily,

gold in the ground, get the better of
one of human race, hide it who will!
High above the hoard there hung, as he also saw,
a standard all woven wonderfully in gold,
the finest of finger-linkages: the effulgence it gave
allowed him to see the surface of the ground
and examine the treasures. No trace of the worm
was to be seen there, for the sword had finished him.

2770 I heard of the plundering of the hoard in the knoll,
that ancient Giant-work, by that one man;
he filled his bosom with such flagons and vessels
as he himself chose; the standard he took also,
best of banners.

           Old Beowulf's sword,
iron of edge, had already struck
the creature who had been keeper of the treasures
for so long an age, employing his fire-blast
in the hoard's defence, flinging out its heat
in the depth of the nights; he died at last, violently.

2780 The envoy made haste in his eagerness to return,
urged on by his prizes. He was pressed by anxiety
as to whether he would find his fearless man,
the lord of the Geats, alive in the open
where he had left him, lacking in strength.
Carrying the treasures, he came upon his prince,
the famous king, covered in blood
and at his life's end; again he began
to sprinkle him with water, until this word's point
broke through the breast-hoard.

           The battle-king spoke,
2790 an aged man in sorrow; he eyed the gold.

'I wish to put in words my thanks
to the King of Glory, the Giver of All,
the Lord of Eternity, for these treasures that I gaze upon,
that I should have been able to acquire for my people
before my death-day an endowment such as this.
My life's full portion I have paid out now
for this hoard of treasure; you must attend the people's
needs henceforward; no further may I stay.
Bid men of battle build me a tomb
2800 fair after fire, on the foreland by the sea
that shall stand as a reminder of me to my people,
towering high above Hronesness
so that ocean travellers shall afterwards name it
Beowulf's barrow, bending in the distance
their masted ships through the mists upon the sea.'

He unclasped the golden collar from his neck,
staunch-hearted prince, and passed it to the thane,
with the gold-plated helmet, harness and arm-ring;
he bade the young spear-man use them well:
2810 'You are the last man left of our kindred,
the house of the Waymundings! Weird has lured
each of my family to his fated end,
each earl through his valour; I must follow them.'

This was the aged man's uttermost word
from the thoughts of his breast; he embraced the pyre's
seething surges; soul left its case,
going its way to the glory of the righteous.

How wretchedly it went with the warrior then,
the younger soldier, when he saw on the ground

2820 his best-beloved at his life's end
suffering miserably! The slayer lay also
bereft of life, beaten down in ruin,
terrible earth-drake. He was unable any longer
to rule the ring-hoard, the writhing serpent,
since the hammers' legacy, hard and battle-scarred,
the iron edges, had utterly destroyed him;
the far-flier lay felled along the ground
beside his store-house, still from his wounds.
He did not mount the midnight air,
2830 gliding and coiling, glorying in his hoard,
flaunting his aspect; he fell to the earth
at the powerful hand of that prince in war.
Not one of the men of might in that land,
however daring in deeds of every kind,
had ever succeeded, from all I have heard,
in braving the venomous breath of that foe
or putting rude hands on the rings in that hall
if his fortune was to find the defender of the barrow
waiting and on his guard. The gaining of the hoard
2840 of beautiful treasure was Beowulf's death;
so it was that each of them attained the end
of his life's lease.

                It was not long then
till they budged from the wood, the battle-shirkers,
ten of them together, those traitors and weaklings
who had not dared deploy their spears
in their own lord's extreme need.
They bore their shields ashamedly,
their armour of war, to where the old man lay.
They regarded Wiglaf. Wearily he sat,
2850 a foot-soldier, at the shoulder of his lord,

trying to wake him with water; but without success.
For all his desiring it, he was unable to hold
his battle-leader's life in this world
or affect anything of the All-Wielder's;
for every man's action was under the sway
of God's judgement, just as it is now.

There was a rough and a ready answer
on the young man's lips for those who had lost their
     nerve.
Wiglaf spoke, Weoxstan's offspring,
2860 looked at the unloved ones with little joy at heart:
'A man who would speak the truth may say with justice
that a lord of men who allowed you those treasures,
who bestowed on you the trappings that you stand there in
— as, at the ale-bench, he would often give
to those who sat in hall both helmet and mail-shirt
as a lord to his thanes, and things of the most worth
that he was able to find anywhere in the world —
that he had quite thrown away and wasted cruelly
all that battle-harness when the battle came upon him.
2870 The king of our people had no cause to boast
of his companions of the guard. Yet God vouchsafed him,
the Master of Victories, that he should avenge himself
when courage was wanted, by his weapon alone.
I was little equipped to act as body-guard
for him in the battle, but, above my own strength,
I began all the same to support my kinsman.
Our deadly enemy grew ever the weaker —
when I had struck him with my sword — less strongly
     welled
the fire from his head. Too few supporters

2880 flocked to our prince when affliction came.
Now there shall cease for your race the receiving of
            treasure,
the bestowal of swords, all satisfaction of ownership,
all comfort of home. Your kinsmen every one,
shall become wanderers without land-rights
as soon as athelings over the world
shall hear the report of how you fled,
a deed of ill fame. Death is better
for any earl than an existence of disgrace!'

He bade that the combat's result be proclaimed in the city
2890 over the brow of the headland; there the band of earls
had sat all morning beside their shields
in heavy spirits, half expecting
that it would be the last day of their beloved man,
half hoping for his return. The rider from the headland
in no way held back the news he had to tell;
as his commission was, he called out over all:
'The Lord of the Geats lies now on his slaughter-bed,
the leader of the Weathers, our loving provider,
dwells in his death-rest through the dragon's power.
2900 Stretched out beside him, stricken with the knife,
lies his deadly adversary. With the edge of the sword
he could not contrive, try as he might,
to wound the monster. Weoxstan's son
Wiglaf abides with Beowulf there,
one earl waits on the other one lifeless;
in weariness of heart he watches by the heads
of friend and foe.
                    The fall of the king,
when it spreads abroad and is spoken of

among the Frisians and the Franks, forebodes a time
2910 of wars for our people. The war against the Hugas
had a hard beginning when Hygelac sailed
into the land of the Frisians with his fleet-army:
there it was that the Hetware hurled themselves upon him
and with their greater strength stoutly compelled
that battle-clad warrior to bow before them;
he fell among the troop, distributed no arms
as lord to the guard. It has not been granted to us since
to receive mercy from the Merovingian king.

Nor can I expect peace or fair dealing
2920 from the Swedish nation; it is no secret
that it was Ongentheow who put an end to the life
of Hrethel's son, Hathkin, by Hrefnawudu
when in their pride the people of the Geats
first made attack upon the fighting Scylfings.
Quickly did the formidable father of Ohthere,
terrible veteran, return that blow,
he cut down the sea-king, recaptured his wife,
the mother of Onela and Ohthere in her youth,
now an aged woman, her ornaments stripped from her.
2930 He then drove after his deadly foes
so that they hid themselves, hard-pressed,
in the Ravenswood, and without a lord.

With his host he besieged those whom swords had left
ailing from their wounds. All through the night
he promised horrors to that unhappy band,
saying that on the morrow he would mutilate them
with the edges of the sword, and set some on the gallows
as sport for the birds. With break of day

what comfort came to those care-oppressed men
2940 when they heard Hygelac's horn and trumpet
giving voice, as that valiant one came up
with the flower of his host, following on their tracks!

The bloody swathe of the Swedes and the Geats
in their slaughterous pursuit could be seen from afar
– how the peoples had stirred up the strife between them.
The earl Ongentheow took the upper ground;
the wise champion went up to his stronghold
in the van of his kinsmen; the veteran grieved,
but he knew the power of the superb Hygelac,
2950 his strength in war; he was not confident
of his resistance, that he could stand against the vikings,
defend his hoard against the fighters from the sea,
his children and his queen. He chose to draw back,
old behind his earth-wall.
                                   Then was the offering of the chase
to the people of the Swedes; sweeping forward,
the standards of Hygelac surged over the camp
as Hrethel's brood broke through the rampart.
Then was Ongentheow the ashen-haired
brought to bay by the brightness of swords
2960 and the king of a nation must kneel as Eofor
singly disposed. It was a desperate blow
that Wulf Wonreding's weapon fetched him,
and at the stroke streams of blood
sprang forth beneath his hair. The hoary-headed Scylfing,
undismayed by this deadly blow,
gave in exchange a graver stroke
as he came round to face him, king of the people.
Wonred's brave son was incapable

of the answer-blow upon the older man,
2970 for the king had cut through the casque on his head,
forced him to bend; he bowed to the earth
marked with blood. Yet he was not marked for death;
it was a keen wound, but he recovered from it.
Then as his brother lay there, the brave Eofor,
Hygelac's follower, fetched his broad sword,
an ancient giant-blade, to the giant-helm of Ongentheow
above his shield, and split it; then the shepherd of the people,
the king, fell down, fatally wounded.

There were many to bind up the brother's wounds;
2980 they raised him at once, now the way was open
and the battlefield had fallen to them.
One sturdy warrior then stripped the other,
took from Ongentheow his iron war-shirt,
his hilted sword and his helmet also,
the old man's accoutrement, and carried it to Hygelac.
He accepted the harness with a handsome promise
of rewards among the people; a promise he kept.
For at his homecoming Hrethel's offspring
rewarded Eofor and Wulf for their assault
2990 with copious treasures. The king of the Geats
handed to each of them a hundred thousand
in lands and linked rings; there was little cause for any
on middle earth to begrudge them these glories earned in
        battle.
He also gave to Eofor his only daughter,
a grace to his home and a guarantee of favour.

It is this feud, this fierce hostility,
this murder-lust between men, I am moved to think,

that the Swedish people will prosecute against us
when once they learn that life has fled
3000 from the lord of the Geats, guardian for so long
of hoard and kingdom, of keen shield-warriors
against every foe. Since the fall of the princes
he has taken care of our welfare, and accomplished yet more
heroic deeds.
    Haste is best now,
that we should go to look on the lord of the people,
then bring our ring-bestower on his road,
escort him to the pyre. More than one portion of wealth
shall melt with the hero, for there's a hoard of treasure
and gold uncounted; a grim purchase,
3010 for in the end it was with his own life
that he bought these rings: which the burning shall devour,
the fire enfold. No fellow shall wear
an arm-ring in his memory; no maiden's neck
shall be enhanced in beauty by the bearing of these rings.
Bereft of gold, rather, and in wretchedness of mind
she shall tread continually the tracks of exile
now that the leader of armies has laid aside his mirth,
his sport and glad laughter. Many spears shall therefore
feel cold in the mornings to the clasping fingers
3020 and the hands that raise them. Nor shall the harper's
    melody
arouse them for battle; and yet the black raven,
quick on the marked men, shall have much to speak of
when he tells the eagle of his takings at the feast
where he and the wolf bared the bodies of the slain'

Such was the rehearsal of the hateful tidings
by that bold messenger; amiss in neither

words nor facts. The war-band arose;
they went unhappily under Earna-ness
to look on the wonder with welling tears.

3030 They found him on the sand, his soul fled,
keeping his resting-place: rings he had given them
in former times! But the final day
had come for the champion; and the chief of the Geats,
the warrior-king, had met his wondrous death.

Stranger the creature they encountered first
in the level place – the loathsome worm
stretched out opposite. Scorched by its own flames
lay the fire-drake in its fatal markings,
and it measured fifty feet as it lay.

3040 He had once been master of the midnight air,
held sweet sway there, and swooped down again
to seek his den; now death held him fast,
he had made his last use of lairs in the earth.

Standing by him there were bowls and flagons,
there were platters lying there, and precious swords,
quite rusted through, as they had rested there
a thousand winters in the womb of earth.

And this gold of former men was full of power,
the huge inheritance, hedged about with a spell:
3050 no one among men was permitted to touch
that golden store of rings unless God Himself,
the true King of Victories, the Protector of mankind,
enabled one He chose to open the hoard,
whichever among men should seem meet to Him.
It was plain to see then that this plan had failed

the creature who had kept these curious things hidden
wrongfully within the wall; the warden had slain
a man like few others; but the feud was straightaway
avenged and wrathfully. It is a wonder to know
3060 where the most courageous of men may come to the end
of his allotted life, and no longer dwell
a man in the mead-hall among companions!

So it was for Beowulf when he embarked on that quarrel,
sought out the barrow-guard; he himself did not know
in what way his parting from the world was to come.
The great princes who had placed the treasure there
had laid on it a curse to last until Doomsday,
that the man who should plunder the place would thereby
commit a crime, and be confined with devils,
3070 tortured grievously in the trammels of hell.
But Beowulf had not looked on the legacy of these men
with too eager an eye, for all its gold.

Wiglaf spoke, Weoxstan's son:
'Many must often endure distress
for the sake of one; so it is with us.
We could not urge any reason
on our beloved king, the keeper of the land,
why he should not approach the protector of the gold
but let him lie where he had long been already
3080 and abide in his den until the end of the world.
He held to his high destiny.
                                        The hoard has been seen
that was acquired at such a cost; too cruel the fate
that impelled the king of the people towards it!
I myself was inside there, and saw all

the wealth of the chamber once my way was open
— little courtesy was shown in allowing me to pass
beneath the earth-wall. I urgently filled
my hands with a huge heap of the treasures
stored in the cave, carried them out
3090 to my lord here. He was alive still
and commanded his wits. Much did he say
in his grief, the old man; he asked me to speak to you,
ordered that on the place of the pyre you should raise
a barrow fitting your friend's achievements;
conspicuous, magnificent, as among men he was
while he could wield the wealth of his stronghold
the most honoured of warriors on the wide earth.

　　Let us now hasten to behold again,
and approach once more that mass of treasures,
3100 awesome under the walls; I shall guide you,
so that from near at hand you may behold sufficiently
the thick gold and the bracelets. Let a bier be made ready,
contrive it quickly, so that when we come out again
we may take up our king, carry the man
beloved by us to his long abode
where he must rest in the Ruler's keeping.'

Then the son of Weoxstan, worthy in battle,
had orders given to owners of homesteads
and a great many warriors, that the governors of the people
3110 from far and wide should fetch in wood
for the hero's funeral pyre.
　　　　　　　　　　　　'Now the flames shall grow dark
and the fire destroy the sustainer of the warriors
who often endured the iron shower

when, string-driven, the storm of arrows
sang over shield-wall, and the shaft did its work,
sped by its feathers, furthered the arrow-head.'

Then in his wisdom Weoxstan's son
called out from the company of the king's own thanes
seven men in all, who excelled among them,
3120　and, himself the eighth warrior, entered in beneath
that unfriendly roof. The front-stepping man
bore in his hand a blazing torch.

When the men perceived a piece of the hoard
that remained unguarded, mouldering there
on the floor of the chamber, they did not choose by lot
who should remove it; undemurring,
as quickly as they could, they carried outside
the precious treasures; and they pushed the dragon,
the worm, over the cliff, let the waves take him
3130　and the flood engulf the guardian of the treasures.
Untold profusion of twisted gold
was loaded onto a wagon, and the warrior prince
borne hoary-headed to Hronesness.

The Geat race then reared up for him
a funeral pyre. It was not a petty mound,
but shining mail-coats and shields of war
and helmets hung upon it, as he had desired.
Then the heroes, lamenting, laid out in the middle
their great chief, their cherished lord.
3140　On top of the mound the men then kindled
the biggest of funeral-fires. Black wood-smoke
arose from the blaze, and the roaring of flames

mingled with weeping. The winds lay still
as the heat at the fire's heart consumed
the house of bone. And in heavy mood
they uttered their sorrow at the slaughter of their lord.

A woman of the Geats in grief sang out
the lament for his death. Loudly she sang,
her hair bound up, the burden of her fear
3150   that evil days were destined her
— troops cut down, terror of armies,
bondage, humiliation. Heaven swallowed the smoke.

Then the Storm-Geat nation constructed for him
a stronghold on the headland, so high and broad
that seafarers might see it from afar.
The beacon to that battle-reckless man
they made in ten days. What remained from the fire
they cast a wall around, of workmanship
as fine as their wisest men could frame for it.
3160   They placed in the tomb both the torques and the jewels,
all the magnificence that the men had earlier
taken from the hoard in hostile mood.
They left the earls' wealth in the earth's keeping,
the gold in the dirt. It dwells there yet,
of no more use to men than in ages before.

Then the warriors rode around the barrow,
twelve of them in all, athelings' sons.
They recited a dirge to declare their grief,
spoke of the man, mourned their king.
3170   They praised his manhood and the prowess of his hands,
they raised his name; it is right a man

should be lavish in honouring his lord and friend,
should love him in his heart when the leading-forth
from the house of flesh befalls him at last.

This was the manner of the mourning of the men of the
        Geats,
sharers in the feast, at the fall of their lord:
they said that he was of all the world's kings
the gentlest of men, and the most gracious,
the kindest to his people, the keenest for fame.

The Fight at Finnsburh

The Fight at Finnsburh, a fragment, is included, as is usual in translations of *Beowulf*, for it helps in understanding what happened at Finn's Stronghold (*Beowulf*, 1067ff.).

The only text of this fragment appears in George Hickes's *Linguarum Veterum Septentrionalium Thesaurus Grammatico-Criticus et Archaeologicus* (Oxoniae, 1705). Hickes found it on a leaf bound up with a collection of homilies in Lambeth Palace library; the leaf has since been lost.

The fragment is the story of a night attack made on a hall, and of the five days' defence made by Hnæf and his men. But why the attack was made, or by whom, would not have been known without the evidence of the Finn episode in *Beowulf*.

The fragment begins in the middle of a speech by a man guarding the door of Hnæf's hall.

    '. . . the horns of the house, hall-gables burning?'

Battle-young Hnæf broke silence:
'It is not the eaves aflame, nor in the east yet
does day break; no dragon flies this way.
It is the soft clashing of claymores you hear
that they carry to the house.

                    Soon shall be the cough of birds,
hoar wolf's howl, hard wood-talk,
shield's answer to shaft.

                          Now shines the moon,
welkin-wanderer. The woes at hand
10   shall bring to the full this folk's hatred for us.

     Awake! on your feet! Who fights for me?
Hold your lindens right, hitch up your courage,
think bravely, be with me at the doors!'
The gold-clad thanes rose, girt on their swords.
Two doubtless soldiers stepped to the door,
Sigeferth and Eaha, with their swords out,
and Ordlaf and Guthlaf to the other door went,
Hengest himself hastening in their steps.

Hearing these adversaries advance on the door
20   Guthere held on to Garulf so he should not
front the rush to force the threshold
and risk his life, whose loss could not be remedied;
but clear above their whispers he called out his
                    demand,
– brave heart – 'Who held the door?'

'My name is Sigeferth, of the Secgan, chief,
known through the seas. I have seen a few fights
and can take on trouble. What you intend for me
your own flesh shall be the first to taste.'

Then swung strokes sounded along the wall;
30   wielded by the brave, the bone-shielding
boss-boards split. Burg-floor spoke,
and Garulf fell at last in the fighting at the door,
Garulf, the first man in the Frisian islands,
son to Guthlaf, and good men lay around,

a pale crowd of corpses. The crows dangled
black and brown. Blades clashing
flashed fire — as though all Finnsburh were ablaze.

Never have sixty swordmen in a set fight
borne themselves more bravely; or better I have not heard
    of.
40   Never was the bright mead better earned
than that which Hnæf gave his guard of youth.

They fought and none fell. On the fifth day
the band was still whole and still held the doors.
Then a wounded warrior went to the side,
said his ring-coat was riven to pieces,
stout hauberk though it was, and that his helm had gone
      through.

The folk's shepherd and shielder asked him
how the braves bore their wounds
and which of the young men . . .

Notes

The Notes try to clear up the more obvious difficulties that may be encountered by a reader of the poem in translation. In addition, a few alternative textual readings or interpretations are briefly mentioned. (See A Note on the Text, p. lxv.) The notes should be supplemented by the information in the Index of Proper Names (p. 133). A general framework is offered in the Introduction.

It should be remembered, as the Note on the Text explains, that line references are to the text of this translation, not to the line-numbering of the original text in modern editions.

1. 'Attend!': The 'oral' beginning offers a retrospect upon the former glory of the Danish royal house. The miraculous arrival of Scyld, eponymous founder of the Scylding dynasty, brings joy to the Danes. The infant found on the shore (like Moses in the bulrushes) becomes the 'shield' of his people and brings them prosperity and security in the form of a son and heir, Beow. Beow ('Beowulf the Dane', 53) is not to be confused with Beowulf the Geat, hero of the poem, introduced at 193. Scyld was also included as an ancestor in tenth-century genealogies of the kings of Wessex.

The richness of Scyld's funeral (lines 26ff.) is not poetic hyperbole, as is shown by the richness and composition of the treasure-hoard in the buried funeral ship found in 1939 at Sutton Hoo, the royal burying ground of the East Anglian dynasty of the Wuffings. The Sutton Hoo ship, which is 27 metres in length, contained a set of magnificent armour and regalia, drinking-horns, bowls from Constantinople, food, drink and money, and also baptismal spoons – but no trace of a body. The ship may be the burial-place, or cenotaph, of Rædwald, the king of the East Angles who maintained pagan and Christian altars, according to Bede, and died *c.* 625. The hoard is now in the British Museum. See R. L. S. Bruce-Mitford *et al.*, *The Sutton Hoo Ship Burial* (British Museum, London, 1975–83; W. Sessions (UK)/State Mutual Book and Periodical Service, New York, 1988). But Scyld's ship is neither buried nor, as in other accounts of Scandinavian funerals, set on fire. It passes into the unknown. See G. N. Garmonsway and J. Simpson, *Beowulf and its Analogues* (Dent and Dutton, London and New York, 1968).

43. 'not less great': i.e. vastly greater, since the child had nothing. Severe understatement, characteristic of Old English poetry.

61. Words missing from the text. 'Ursula' is invented. Other records give Healfdene's daughter's name as Yrse.

81b–82a. 'unkindled the torch-flame/that turned it to ashes': Literally, 'it awaited the destructive surges of hostile fire'. A dark allusion to the eventual burning down of Heorot by the Heathobards. Hrothgar is to marry his daughter Freawaru to Ingeld the Heathobard. But, as Beowulf foretells at 2019ff., the Heathobards will not forget that Ingeld's father, Froda, had been killed by the Danes. That stories of Ingeld were well known (and that the audience might be expected to take the point of this allusion) is suggested by the letter of Alcuin to a Mercian bishop in the year 797: 'Let the words of God be read at episcopal dinners; there it is proper that a reader should be heard, not a harper, the counsels of the Fathers [of the Church], not the songs of the heathens. What has Ingeld to do with Christ?' Clerical tastes and lay tastes overlapped.

85–113. The Creation, Cain and Abel, and the Giants are taken from the opening chapters of Genesis, the first book of the Bible. For the comparable story of Cædmon see D. H. Farmer (ed.), *Bede's Ecclesiastical History of the English People* etc., trans. L. Sherley-Price, rev. edn (Penguin Books, Harmondsworth, 1990) pp. 248–51.

140. Grendel is called 'the new hall-thane' with irony: the poet carefully records usurpations of the rights of ownership, territory or hospitality. Hearth-companions should sleep by the hearth, not 'among the outer buildings' (139).

155. 'The blood-price was unpaid' – by the less than human Grendel. The civilized way of settling a feud was by a compensatory payment of *wergild*, a slain man's worth in money according to rank.

178. 'a heathen hope': The poet marks the gulf between his present Christian audience and the heathenism of their ancestral homelands. Bede, writing earlier than the poet of *Beowulf*, records lapses into paganism in bad times.

193. Beowulf is introduced as 'one of *Hygelac*'s followers': his name is held back, as with Heorot, Grendel, Wulfgar.

305. 'Fierce guards' translates *grimmon*, emended from MS *grummon*; which if retained yields 'warlike hearts became fierce'.

459. Nothing is known of the 'feud that [Beowulf's] father set off' between the Geats and the Wylfings. The young Hrothgar paid the *wergild* for Heatholaf, something evidently beyond the means of Edgetheow or his people. Beowulf repays Hrothgar by ending the Grendel-feud.

489–90. 'attend': Beowulf could be asked to 'reveal' rather than to 'attend' if *on sæl meoto* is retained and understood as 'unseal your thoughts'.

499. Hrothgar's spokesman *Unferth* provokes a 'flyting' or verbal combat by doubting the word of Hrothgar's guest. This gives Beowulf an opportunity to disclose himself as a slayer of underwater monsters, which paves the way for the later Mere-fight and the feat of swimming by which Beowulf escapes from Friesland. Unferth's provocation is a convention; compare that of Laodamas in the *Odyssey*. The name may mean 'Un-peace'; Unferth is anti-peace in that he has killed his own kindred (587ff.; cf. Cain, Hathkin, Heremod, Hrothulf, Onela). He later offers Beowulf his sword, Hrunting, for the Mere-fight; Hrunting's failure again gives Beowulf an opportunity to show valour and magnanimity.

515. 'the Spear-Man' – the sea. Neptune's trident?

569. 'Day': The sun and its light betoken glory for Beowulf at 220–21, 1570 and 1963.

612. *Wealhtheow*, Hrothgar's queen, is a good hostess. She moves through the hall among the young men and the older men, offering the cup, in the way prescribed in the Old English Maxims or Gnomic Verses (see Michael Alexander (ed. and trans.), *Earliest English Poems*, pp. 65–6). In the patriarchal warrior aristocracy of the poem, women, valued for the peaceful virtues, appear incidentally as beautiful, as companions of the bed, or as shrews. They are more conspicuous as queens and hostesses; as 'peace-weavers', when a daughter is given in marriage in order to heal a dynastic feud, as with Hildeburgh or Freawaru; and as widows – Hildeburgh again. Accepting the hospitable cup, Beowulf makes on it the third of his four Grendel-vows.

668. Beowulf is appointed by God 'to cope with the monster'. Line 670 has a characteristic apposition.

681. Grendel's inability to use a sword, like his lack of table-manners, marks his incomplete humanity. Part man, part monster, his exact appearance is left indefinite. He is huge and weapon-proof, has a hand with talons like steel, a magic glove and hellish eyes. He is a demon and a wild animal, but he is also human, a descendant of Cain. Glam, with his elbows on the cross-beam looking down at Grettir in bed, is a more definite figure. See Denton Fox and Hermann Palsson (trans.), *Grettir's Saga* (University of Toronto Press, Toronto, 1974, repr. 1981).

740. Why does Beowulf allow Grendel to devour his companion, later named as Handscio? Perhaps Handscio is a sacrificial figure, like Protesilaos, Elpenor or Palinurus – or the first Viking to step on to the causeway in *The Battle of Maldon* at line 77 (Michael Alexander, *Earliest English Poems*, p. 104).

742. *Syn* may well mean 'sinful' rather than 'huge', for drinking (the soul's) blood was abhorrent to Christians.

780. 'might undo that . . . hall': The apparent indestructibility of the hall may be partly magical. Intricate art is accorded wonder in *Beowulf*: see the building of the dragon's barrow and of Beowulf's barrow; the manufacture of weapons, armour, cups and adornments; and the skill of the *scop* – the artificer-poet (e.g. 89ff., 866ff.). Well-made things can be handed down, and the undoing of Heorot would be the undoing of Danish society.

813b–814a. 'hateful to each/was the breath of the other': Many of the clinching points of *Beowulf* are made in such juxtapositions, which are hard to translate.

824. The notion of 'cleansing' is also expressed at 432, 1175, 1620 and 2350.

828. 'made good his boast': Pride in the performance of a vow is regarded as justified.

866bff. 'Or a fellow of the king's': The most valuable of the poem's descriptions of impromptu verse composition. At 870a, *sothe gebunden*, 'made in the measure', refers to metre and alliteration, rightly bound together.

874. The lay about Beowulf's new exploit is followed by a recital of the deeds of *Sigemund*, told very summarily: 'He was by far the most famous of adventurers', 897. One point of this elevating comparison with the great Germanic hero may be the difference between the dragon-fights of Sigemund and of Beowulf: Sigemund kills his dragon alone 'under the grey rock'(887), and takes the gold away in his boat. There was a curse upon this gold, from which Sigemund eventually died. Beowulf will die in his dragon-fight, and gold will be buried with him. So the compliment conceals a tragic irony. In later tradition, the dragon-fight is attributed to Siegfried, in the Old Icelandic *Volsungasaga* and the Middle High German *Nibelungenlied*.

900–14. Whereas Sigemund is a great hero, *Heremod* is here introduced as a foil to Beowulf. Scyld's predecessor, he is presented as a tyrannical Danish king, who notoriously went to the bad after a glorious youth, most unlike Beowulf. This ethical comparison is underlined when in 1708ff. Hrothgar holds him up to Beowulf as a dreadful warning.

979ff. 'The son of Edgelaf', Unferth, is reduced to unwonted silence by the sight of Grendel's arm, hand, fingers and nails.

1006. 'The body shall sleep' in death after the feast of life. A natural symbolism, made actual at 1250a.

1016. Hrothulf, the son of Hrothgar's brother Halga, has some share in the rule of Denmark, though subsidiary to his uncle the king. 'Falsity in those days' hints at later disloyalty. Hrothulf succeeded Hrothgar. A Danish tradition suggests that he killed Hrethric, Hrothgar's son.

1024. 'no cause to be ashamed': An understatement – Beowulf gloried in his prizes, which include Hrothgar's battle-saddle, and perhaps Hrothgar's father's sword, if *brand Healfdenes*, 1019b, is taken literally and in the accusative. The translation 'the son of Healfdene' takes *brand* as nominative and metaphorical: Hrothgar as Healfdene's chief warrior.

1067ff. The lay of Finn. Part of the story summarized here is told in the fragmentary Anglo-Saxon poem, *The Fight at Finnsburh*, or the *Finnsburh Fragment* (p. 114). The story in outline – reduced to order – is as follows:

Hnæf, a Dane (or 'Half-Dane'), is visiting his sister Hildeburgh, who is married to Finn, the king of the Frisians (some of whose followers were Jutes). The Frisians treacherously attack the Danes in the night, and kill both Hnæf and Hildeburgh's son. The surviving Danes, led by Hengest, force Finn to accept a compromise whereby the Danes are to become followers of Finn on equal terms with the Frisians. To serve one's lord's slayer is flat against the Germanic code, and the exile Hengest cannot 'decline the accustomed remedy' (1141) when the son of Hunlaf places a famous sword across his knees. He is bound to take vengeance for Hnæf. Guthlaf and Oslaf, who have been to Denmark and returned again, taunt Finn with his treachery and provoke the final fight. Finn is slain, Hildeburgh taken home; vengeance has successfully been taken by the Danes. At a cost.

The moral would seem to be Beowulf's remark at 2028–30 that 'when a lord is dead/it is seldom the slaying-spear sleeps for long –/seldom indeed – dear though the bride may be'. Hildeburgh and Freawaru are Danish brides whose marriages fail to mend historic feuds, because the universal remedy (1141) is the law of vengeance.

1106. 'The pyre': *Ad.* If MS *Ath* is retained, translate: 'The oath was performed', in which case the gold from (Finn's) hoard (1107) would be *wergild* for Hnæf.

1158–67. The revelry and rejoicing continue; but the tableau of the patriarch Hrothgar supported by Hrothulf and Unferth inspires little confidence after a tale such as we have just heard. The doubts cast on Hrothulf's future and Unferth's past are borne out in Wealhtheow's speech. Lines 1161–7 are six-stress lines, used at solemn moments.

1167–89. Wealhtheow raises the question whether Hrothulf will remember his uncle Hrothgar's kindness when he is gone. The audience may reflect on how Beowulf repays the kindness that Hrothgar and Hrethel had shown him as a child. The tableau of Beowulf between the young Scyldings contrasts with the earlier trio.

1194–1213. The collar is second only to the Brosings' or Brisings' necklace. In later Old Norse tradition, Hama stole from King Eormenric the Ostrogoth a necklace which the Brising fire-dwarves had originally made for the goddess Freya. In the thirteenth-century *Thrithrek's Saga*, Heimir

(Hama) finally becomes a monk; in line 1202b 'made his name forever' could alternatively be rendered 'chose a lasting reward'. As Heimir presented his necklace to the monastery, this famous prize had an ending unlike that of the collar here presented to Beowulf.

The comparison may have some other purpose, but it is made clear that Hygelac wore this collar on a fatal expedition undertaken *for wlenco*, out of pride. Beowulf gives the collar at 2171 to Hygelac's wife, Hygd. Thus, before we hear the applause at the presentation of the collar to Beowulf, we are shown that it will be tragically wasted.

1215ff. If the interpretations offered above are correct, Wealhtheow's diplomatic speech requesting Beowulf to protect her sons betrays a concern about their future. Tragic irony also attends her joy in Heorot's regained harmony, which is about to be shattered by the killing of Ashhere.

1239. *Beorscealca sum*, 'a notable one among those feasting men', does not suggest Beowulf. The poet later reveals that Beowulf slept elsewhere.

1257. The introduction of *Grendel's Mother* starts another cycle of destruction and defence, another stage in the feud: the descent from Cain and the Grendel-fight are rehearsed again because the same thing is happening in the same revengeful pattern. Cf. Denton Fox and Hermann Palsson (trans.), *Grettir's Saga*, chapters 64–6.

1279. 'A sudden change' – *edhwyrft* – is the characteristic movement by which the wrestling-match between good and evil progresses. Cf. *gewrixl*, 'a fresh sorrow', 1302, and *wyrp*, 'a turning', 1314.

1303–5. 'an evil bargain': Reciprocity is maintained – Grendel kills Handscio, Beowulf kills Grendel and keeps his hand; Grendel's mother kills Ashhere and takes the hand, Beowulf kills Grendel's mother. He brings back Grendel's head as war spoil in exchange for Ashhere's head.

1322. *Ashhere* is the ideal counsellor. *Beowulf* tends to put traditional generic character types to edifying use. The coastguard is a good coastguard; but Wulfgar, Ashhere and Wiglaf are role-models. Cf. Spenser's letter to Ralegh in dedication of *The Faerie Queene*.

1330. If MS *hwæther* is retained, Hrothgar does not know 'whether' Grendel's mother has gone back again.

1356–75. Literary descriptions of hell are thought to have influenced this landscape. An early Latin apocryphal work, *The Vision of St Paul*, has many of the same features, and was the ultimate source also of St Paul's vision of hell in a tenth-century homily (*Blickling Homilies*, 16), which has parallels with the *Beowulf* passage. Compare also Denton Fox and Hermann Palsson (trans.), *Grettir's Saga*. The description, which has natural elements in fearsomely unnatural combination, recalls the atmospherics of *Macbeth* rather than a physical topography. The Mere is at once a fenland pool above a hall lit by fire, a cave behind a mountain torrent, an arm of the sea surrounded by cliffs, and a lake burning with fire and brimstone (Apocalypse 21:8). It is the entrance to hell.

1383–88. 'better to . . . avenge': Beowulf's response is classic heroism, not Christianity.

1420. 'the head of Ashhere': The unnatural horror of the unburied head, of the blood on the water and of the repulsive sea-monsters is banished magically by the 'bright phrases' of the horn (cf. the effects of Hygelac's horn at 2940). The Gothic grisliness of their 'guest' is likewise quelled by the splendour of the hero's arming. Unferth is once more a foil.

1512. The underwater 'hall' has no hearth but an unnatural fire. The progress of the fight is symmetrical: after Beowulf's sword fails, he throws her to the ground; she then throws him, but her knife fails. Beowulf, like Grendel, is immune to swords, and ordinary swords are useless to him. God provides a giant-sword 'as soon as the Geat regained his feet' (1555).

1537. If MS *eaxl*, shoulder, is emended to *feaxe*, hair, alliteration is improved.

1585. 'lay at rest': Grendel is dead. The metaphor of sleep is common in the poem. Cf. also *The Dream of the Rood* (Michael Alexander, *Earliest English Poems*, p. 103). Decapitation proved death. Danes decapitated King Edmund, and (at Maldon) Ealdorman Bryhtnoth.

1602. 'staring at the pool': Both parties think the blood is Beowulf's. The Danes go home, their guests stay on. Compare construction and situation with 2890–94, where the experienced warriors are right. Cf. also 1871–2.

1649. 'they eyed it well': Compare 1421, 1439. Also *Macbeth*, Act III, Scene 4.

1688. 'the primal strife' carved on the hilt is probably Cain's fratricide, though the destruction of the Giants in the Flood refers to Genesis 6:4–6 (cf. *Beowulf* 112–13). The owner's name was often engraved on a sword. For whom the sword was made (1695–7) is the sort of question which preoccupied Sir Thomas Browne in his *Urn Burial*.

1699–1783. Hrothgar's speech of congratulation to Beowulf contains a substantial warning against the self-satisfied enjoyment of worldly prosperity, illustrated by the career of Heremod and perhaps by the events of his own reign. Heremod's meanness and cruelty are typified by the drunken murder of his table-companions. Hrothgar himself is not guilty of pride or closefistedness; his prosperity passes, and in age, after a fifty-year reign, 'grief sprang from joy' (1774). The same reversal is to happen to Beowulf. The moral psychology of the homily seems Christian at 1739–46, but its general tenor resembles that of *The Consolation of Philosophy* of the Roman philosopher Boethius (d. 524), translated by King Alfred the Great (d. 899).

1878. 'Beowulf went': In this poem of strong contrasts there is none more characteristic than that between the presageful grief of the aged Hrothgar at their parting and Beowulf's youthful joy in setting out for home.

In his moments of glory Beowulf is seen striding along in the sunlight, never more unconsciously and vigorously than here. The voyages are the most Homeric passages in the poem in their unclouded briskness and their palindromic symmetry. Launching and landing mirror each other, like sunrise and sunset. In the deployment of the coastguards, of the armed marching men, and the sighting of land, the poet seems to put oral traditions of composition to conscious use.

1923. 'a handsome hall': After Hrothgar and Wealhtheow, Hygelac and Hygd seem somewhat pinched. Geatland, weaker than Denmark, shows us the heroic life from the other side.

1929b–60. Modthryth and *Offa*. The contrast drawn between Hygd and Modthryth (or Thryth, the text is ambiguous) recalls, in substance and in style, that which Hrothgar draws between Beowulf and King Heremod, who kills his table-companions (1711). A queen should be a 'peace-weaver' (1939) like Hygd, not a tyrant. Offa is king of the Angles in Angeln, their continental homeland. He is the legendary ancestor of the historical Offa, the famous eighth-century king of Mercia. The compliments here paid to Offa of Angeln have suggested that the poet of *Beowulf* wished indirectly to compliment Offa of Mercia.

1966. 'Ongentheow's conqueror': Hygelac is the slayer of Ongentheow since he is the lord of Eofor, who killed the Swedish king (2958ff.).

2019. 'Hrothgar's daughter': One surprise in Beowulf's recital is his presentation of Freawaru rather than Wealhtheow as the hostess of Heorot. Her introduction allows Beowulf to voice his doubts about the marrying off of daughters to heal dynastic feuds; Hrothgar does not seem to have learned from the story of Hildeburgh's marriage to Finn. Heorot itself is eventually to be burned down in vengeance for the killing of Froda, the father of Ingeld, Freawaru's husband (see note to 81b–82a), though Beowulf confines himself to imagining the beginning of this stage of the feud. In 2034, 'the pride and daring of Denmark' takes *dryht-bearn* as plural, denoting the Danes attending on Freawaru, but the word could be singular, denoting one of her wedding-attendants. The 'old spear-warrior' plays the part of prompter, like the son of Hunlaf at Finnsburh. 'The other' (2060) is the son of Withergyld; after his act of revenge he conceals himself in the Heathobard lands. The wearer of Withergyld's sword does not awake from his sleep after the wedding-feast. Beowulf's misgivings are well founded: the Heathobard feud with Hrothgar was to become legendary.

2084. 'A glove': The trolls of Scandinavian folklore often carried such a glove. Grendel's glove was not mentioned earlier; nor was Handscio's name given. Beowulf's 'sluggish youth' and Hygelac's efforts to persuade him not to go to Denmark also came as a surprise. We should not expect the consistency of a whodunnit in a protean tale full of wonders, where the detail offered is highly selective. Did Beowulf marry Hygd? We shall never know.

2105–14. The 'veteran of the Scyldings' is taken as referring to Hrothgar, as is 'the seasoned warrior' (2111). The alternative, that Beowulf here refers to two or three storytellers, is unlikely.

2157. Heorogar gave the armour to his brother rather than to his son. In Scandinavian tradition, Heoroweard was to slay his cousin Hrothulf.

2164. 'matching as apples': *æppel-fealuwe*. *Fealo* is an adjective used for apples, horses, waves, paths and fallow land – things which vary in the amount of light they reflect.

2176ff. Beowulf heeds Hrothgar's advice: his career is the reverse of Heremod's, and, unlike Hrothulf, he proves a loyal nephew to his king. Yet time is to bring a 'reversal' (2188) to him also.

2194. 'seven thousand hides': A hide was a measure of land, enough to support a *ceorl* and his household.

2199. Here begins the second part of *Beowulf*. The action moves forward fifty years, passing over the death of kings (recalled later) to the end of the reign of King Beowulf. The *wrecca* or adventurer has become an old king, like Hrothgar, and is confronted with his greatest adversary, the dragon. The dragon attacks the Geats because his hoard has been rifled by a slave; the slave had to rob the hoard so as to appease his lord's anger. The hoard is the treasure of an entire race, now extinct. We later hear that it has a curse attached to it.

2205. Here begins a damaged leaf of the MS. The text to line 2250 is incomplete and conjectural in some places. The speech given to the 'last survivor' (2245–65) is a sustained example of the poem's habit of metonymy: the heroic way of life is represented in terms of its material prizes. Cf. *The Ruin* and the end of *The Wanderer* (Michael Alexander, *Earliest English Poems*, pp. 2 and 50).

2323. The poem makes several attempts to 'explain' the dragon and the hoard, inherited features of the story. Beowulf's immediate move to avenge the burning down of his hall is another given feature. He fears he may have angered God, but it is stressed that such dark thoughts were 'unaccustomed' (2331). Motivation is *post hoc*. The action is henceforward counterpointed by ever more substantial flashbacks.

2353–93. 'when Hygelac was slain': An expansion of the deaths mentioned in 1201–13. After Hygelac's death in Friesland (against the Hetware, Hugas and Merovingian Franks) Beowulf declines Hygd's offer of the kingdom. The ideal uncle, he serves Heardred as he had served his father. But in the Second Swedish War (recounted first) Heardred is killed by Onela, the uncle of Eanmund and Eadgils, whom he has deprived of the Swedish throne; Heardred pays the penalty for offering them hospitality. Beowulf later helps Eadgils overthrow Onela.

2359. 'into the ocean he leapt': The verb means to go, ascend, step up. Some render this 'embark', preferring Beowulf to row or sail the hundreds of miles to Geatland rather than, as the text says, to swim across. Thirty mail-coats represent heroic victories, rather than a logistical problem.

2377. 'Ohthere's sons': Eanmund and Eadgils.

2382. 'Hygelac's son': Heardred.

2425–68. 'that open-handed lord': Hrethel married his only daughter to Edgetheow and brought up his grandson Beowulf like one of his own sons; Beowulf in return serves these sons loyally (a contrast with Hrothulf in Denmark). The patriarch Hrethel dies of grief after his eldest son Herebeald has accidentally been shot dead by the second son, Hathkin. Fratricide cannot be settled by *wergild* or by vengeance; Hrethel's plight is compared with that of a man whose only son has been executed as a criminal. In neither case was there a role for either *wergild* or vengeance. Hrethel was nevertheless able to leave the land of the Geats to his remaining sons, as is pointed out by Beowulf, who has no son.

2469–86. 'On Hrethel's death': Hathkin's fratricidal arrow leads to the tragic death of Hrethel, which in its turn is the signal for the Swedes to begin the First Swedish War. Ohthere and Onela, sons of the Swedish patriarch Ongentheow, ambush the Geats. A Geatish punitive expedition succeeds, but their king, Hathkin, is killed by Ongentheow; who in his turn is killed by Hathkin's brother, Hygelac, or rather by Hygelac's retainer, Eofor. This episode is treated fully at 2920–94.

2481. 'But came the morrow, and a kinsman': Hygelac. Although it is Hygelac's retainer Eofor who performs the deed, Hygelac is credited with avenging Hathkin by killing Ongentheow.

2496. 'this blade': The sword Beowulf uses, later called Nailing, seems to be taken from Dayraven, the champion of the Frankish Hugas and the slayer of Hygelac. Dayraven is the only man whom we know to have been killed by Beowulf – with his bare hands, he tells his companions. The name Bee-wolf is often taken to mean Bear.

2523. 'worked out at the wall': Compare Sigemund's 'grey rock' at 887, Ashhere's head on the 'hoary rock' at 1414, and the 'grey stone' of the dragon's hoard at 2742.

2593ff. Comparison has been made between the 'band of picked companions' and the twelve apostles, and between Wiglaf and St Peter, but not between the slave and Judas. *The Battle of Maldon*, line 185, is nearer: the companions flee to the wood (Michael Alexander, *Earliest English Poems*, p. 107). Wiglaf is, like Sigemund's Fitela, 'the young companion' – an ideal thane, kinsman and confidant. His father Weoxstan, fighting for the Swedish king Onela, killed Eanmund in the Second Swedish War, and was given Eanmund's sword. Weoxstan, a Scylfing and therefore a Swede, leaves Eanmund's sword to Wiglaf 'among the Geats'. Weoxstan, Wiglaf and Beowulf all belong to the Waymundings, perhaps a family of the Geat–Swedish border. Wiglaf's words give classic expression of the ethical ideal of the thane in heroic society. His conduct is both exemplary and exceptional.

2681-2. 'his hand was too strong./I have heard that any sword': This is a rationalization of a folklore trait connected with Beowulf's name (see note to 2496). When Beowulf was Heardred's champion, he used Nailing. He used no sword against Dayraven. But normal swords are of no use to him against abnormal foes: he used no sword against Grendel. Hrunting fails against the ogress, Nailing against the dragon. He is provided with a giant-sword to kill Grendel's mother and to cut off Grendel's head. The unavailingness of swords, shields and armour also becomes a general theme of the poem.

2726ff. 'I would now wish to give': Beowulf in his first dying speech rejoices in the thought of the protection he has given his people and in his blameless discharge of the duties of lordship; he has sworn a wrongful oath 'very rarely' (i.e. never); he has not committed the supreme crime, the killing of kinsmen. His desire to look on the gold he has won has sometimes been construed – or misconstrued – as blameworthy.

2761–3. 'Treasure can easily': The homiletic warning against avarice does not – strictly – seem to apply to Beowulf, Wiglaf, the Geats or even the slave. The taboo on grave-robbing, expressed in the curse on the gold, also seems of general rather than particular application. Heroic death is rewarded with heroic glory – gold – which the hero's people return to the ground in tribute to him.

2799ff. There is a remarkable resemblance between this and the account of the funeral pyre of Achilles and Patroclus described at *Odyssey* xxiv, 80ff.

2817. 'the glory of the righteous': Such a translation accords salvation to Beowulf. Syntax allows *sothfæstra dom* several possible meanings: 'the renown [*or* judgement] of [*or* passed upon] those who are fast in truth [secular *or* Christian]'. As George Jack observes in his edition of *Beowulf*, 'in collocation with *gewat sawol secean* the phrase is more naturally taken as Christian in sense, denoting either the glory that belongs in eternity to the just (subjective genitive), or the judgement of God upon the just (objective genitive)'.

2897. ' "The Lord of the Geats lies now on his slaughter-bed" ': Like everything subsequent to the double death, the messenger's speech looks forward to imminent invasion by either the Franks or the Swedes and to the catastrophic defeat of the Geats, who are now without Beowulf's protection. This 128-line speech sums up the latter part of the poem, as Hrothgar's parting words (1699–1783) point the moral of the events of his reign. After another allusion to Hygelac's fall in Friesland, we at last get a full picture of the First Swedish War. In the most vivid sequence in the poem, the logic of the feud is given clear expression in open narrative rather than allusion; in comparison with this, some other episodes seem contrived for their exemplary value. After the 'bloody swathe' (2943) and the killing of the dragon-like Ongentheow (at the hands of two men), the messenger's conclusion at 2996 is irresistible.

2910–18. 'The war against the Hugas': Hygelac's attack on the Frisians, Hugas and Hetware is presented here as provoking the king of the Merovingian Franks; these peoples lived on his north-west frontier. At 1205 the poet described Hygelac's prideful raid on Frisia as asking for trouble; now the Geat messenger criticizes the arrogance of Hathkin's attack on the Swedes.

2935. 'he promised horrors': Ongentheow's threats recall the pagan practice of stabbing and hanging enemies in sacrifice to Odin.

3009ff. 'a grim purchase': The dearly bought gold is to be sacrificed with the body in tribute; the Geats will not profit by it, they will become the boast of the raven to the eagle. These birds, with the wolf, are the beasts of battle who feast on the slain.

3048–54; 3066–72. 'this gold of former men': A curse traditionally attached to buried treasure. Its applicability to the slave, the dragon, the various Geats, the last survivor, or to his people who took the gold from the ground (2247) is not clear. Beowulf certainly dies, but the possibility that he is damned seems to be excluded by 2817, 3053–4 and 3071–2.

3071–2. The comment after Beowulf's death is obscure. Perhaps: 'Earlier he had by no means realized the gold-giving munificence of the owner more (i.e. sufficiently) clearly.' The identity of the 'owner' of the hoard, whose munificence Beowulf now sees more clearly than before, is unclear. The comment seems to be unconnected with the curse.

3076–81. That efforts were made to dissuade Beowulf (not previously mentioned, but cf. 1990–95) is not meant to suggest that he was hubristic. Simply to blame Beowulf here, or Bryhtnoth at Maldon or Roland at Roncesvalles, is to misunderstand heroic poetry.

3088. 'heap' of . . . treasures': Compare Scyld's funeral at 26ff.

3111–16. ' "Now the flames shall grow dark" ': Wiglaf observes with magnificent periphrasis that fire will now do what no iron has been able to do.

3123–8. The speed with which the eight men eagerly rifled the hoard seems due to hostility (3162) rather than pleasure or fear.

3134ff. 'The Geat race then reared up for him': There are two stages – after a funeral similar to that of Hnæf, the ashes, together with the gold from the hoard, are placed in a barrow.

3147–79. This final leaf of the MS is badly damaged. 'The unnamed Geatish woman, uttering a song of lament, is best understood as fulfilling a traditional function of ritual mourner within the funeral ceremony' (George Jack, *Beowulf*).

3165. 'of no more use to men than in ages before': That the gold in the earth is as useless to men as it had been before has an irony influenced by Christian attitudes. But as pagan grave-goods were dedicated for use in the afterlife, it has been suggested that such buried treasure might have 'supernatural associations of a potentially baleful kind' which made them unusable by the living (see George Jack, *Beowulf*, p. 210).

3178–9. The warriors' epitaph uses four terms of praise which show that Beowulf integrated his heroic eagerness for fame with the ideal of service to his people.

This map gives a somewhat speculative idea of the probable locations, at the time in which *Beowulf* is set (fifth and sixth centuries), of the peoples featuring in the poem. Heorot is marked in Zealand, at Lejre near Roskilde, where the kings of the Scylding dynasty are said to be buried.

The continental Saxons (not mentioned in *Beowulf*) lived south of the Heathobards. It was from these shores that Angles, Saxons, Jutes, Frisians and Franks came to settle in Britain in the fifth and sixth centuries, followed, in the ninth and tenth centuries, by Danes and Vikings.

Index of Proper Names

ABEL Killed by Cain, his brother. Genesis 4:8.

ALFHERE Kinsman of Wiglaf.

ASHHERE Hrothgar's counsellor, Yrmenlaf's brother.

BEANSTAN Breca's father.

BEOW or BEOWULF Danish king, son of Scyld, father of Healfdene.

BEOWULF Son of Edgetheow the Waymunding; nephew of Hygelac.

BRECA Son of Beanstan; chief of the Brondings.

BRISINGS See 1194n.

BRONDINGS Unidentified tribe.

CAIN Killer of Abel, his younger brother; first fratricide; father of all monsters.

DANES Hrothgar's people, also called Scyldings.

DAYRAVEN Champion of the Franks.

EADGILS Swedish prince, son of Ohthere, brother of Eanmund. See 2353n.

EANMUND Swedish prince, son of Ohthere, younger brother of Eadgils.

EARNA-NESS A headland in Geatland. (*Earn*: eagle.)

EDGELAF Father of Unferth.

EDGETHEOW A Waymunding who married the only daughter of the Geat king Hrethel; slayer of Heatholaf; Beowulf's father.

EDGEWELA A Danish king otherwise unknown.

EOFOR Geat warrior, slayer of Ongentheow; son of Wonred; brother of Wulf; husband of Hygelac's daughter.

EOMER Son of Offa the Angle.

EORMENRIC The famous king of the East Goths.

FINN King of the East Frisians, ruler also of the Jutes; son of Folcwalda; husband of Hildeburgh. See 1067n.

FITELA Nephew (and son) of Sigemund.

FOLCWALDA Father of Finn.

FRANKS The Franks, under the Merovingian kings; also called Hugas; the Frisians and Hetware are their tributaries; enemies of the Geats. See 2353n.

FREAWARU Hrothgar's daughter; to marry Ingeld.

FRISIANS The Frisians, whether East (Finn's people) or West (tributaries of the Franks).

FRODA King of the Heathobards, father of Ingeld. Killed by the Danes.

GARMUND Father of Offa the Angle.

GEATS Beowulf's people, inhabitants of modern Gotarike in Southern Sweden. Also called Weather-Geats.

GIFTHAS An East Germanic tribe.

GRENDEL Monster killed by Beowulf; descendant of Cain.

GUTHLAF Danish follower of Hnæf, then of Hengest.

HALF-DANES Hnæf's people, tributaries of the Danes. Possibly Jutes.

HALGA Younger brother of Hrothgar; father of Hrothulf.

HAMA Hero who escaped from Eormenric with the Brising necklace.

HANDSCIO A companion of Beowulf on his visit to Heorot.

HARETH Father of Hygd.

HATHKIN Second son of Hrethel, whom he succeeds, having accidentally killed his elder brother Herebeald. Killed by Ongentheow.

HEALFDENE King of the Danes, son of Beowulf the Dane; father of Heorogar, Hrothgar, Halga and 'Ursula'.

HEARDRED Geat king, son of Hygelac and Hygd. Killed by Onela.

HEATHOBARDS Ingeld's people, enemies of the Danes.

HEATHOLAF A Wylfing, killed by Edgetheow.

HELMINGS Wealhtheow's family.

HEMMING Kinsman of Offa and of Eomer.

HENGEST Leader of the Danes (Half-Danes) after Hnæf's death. Hengest the Jute who conquered Kent may be the same man.

HEOROGAR Danish king, Hrothgar's elder brother.

HEOROT Hrothgar's hall. Its site was probably near modern Lejre, Roskilde, Zealand. (*Heorot*: hart – a royal beast, to be seen on the sceptre found at Sutton Hoo.)

HEOROWEARD Heorogar's son; he did not succeed him, perhaps because of his youth.

HEREBEALD Hrethel's eldest son; killed by Hathkin.

HEREMOD Danish tyrant. (*Here*: war; *mod*: mind). See 900n.

HERERIC Heardred's uncle. Possibly Hygd's brother.

HETWARE Frankish tributaries.

HILDEBURGH Wife of Finn; daughter of Hoc; sister of Hnæf.

HNÆF Son of Hoc; brother of Hildeburgh; leader of the Half-Danes.

HOC Father of Hnæf and Hildeburgh.

HREFNAWUDU 'Ravenswood', the Swedish forest where Ongentheow killed Hathkin.

HREOSNABEORGH A hill in Geatland.

HRETHEL King of the Geats, Hygelac's father.

HRETHRIC Son of Hrothgar and Wealhtheow; elder brother of Hrothmund. In tradition, killed by Hrothulf.

HRONESNESS Headland in Geatland. (*Hron*: whale.)

HROTHGAR King of the Danes.

HROTHMUND Hrothgar's son, Hrethric's brother.

HROTHULF Son of Halga; Hrothgar's nephew. See 1016n.

HRUNTING Unferth's sword.

HUGAS A Frankish people, attacked by Hygelac.

HUNLAF Father of one of Hnæf's followers.

HYGD Hygelac's wife, Hareth's daughter.

HYGELAC King of the Geats, Beowulf's uncle. Fell in a raid on the Frisians and the Franks in about the year 521.

INGELD Son of Froda; prince of the Heathobards; husband of Freawaru.

INGWINE A name for the Danes.

MEROVINGIAN, THE King of the Franks.
MODTHRYTH Wife of Offa of Angeln. 1929n.

NAILING The sword Beowulf took from Dayraven.

OFFA King of the Angles in Angeln. Ancestor of Offa of Mercia.
OHTHERE Son of Ongentheow the Swede; elder brother of Onela; father
    of Eanmund and Eadgils.
ONELA Ohthere's brother and successor; husband of Ursula.
ONGENTHEOW Swedish king, father of Ohthere and Onela; slayer of
    Hathkin.
OSLAP Danish follower of Hengest.

RAVENSWOOD See Hrefnawudu.

SCYLD Founder of the Danish royal house, the Scyldings. See note to
    line 1.
SCYLDINGS Descendants of Scyld; the Danish royal family; hence Danes
    in general.
SCYLFINGS The Swedish royal family; hence Swedes in general.
SHEFING Son of Sheaf.
SIGEMUND Son of Wæls; father and uncle of Fitela; conqueror of the
    dragon Fafnir. See 873n.
SWEDES The Swedes of east central Sweden, northern neighbours of the
    Geats.
SWERTING Hygelac's mother's father.

UNFERTH Son of Edgelaf; Hrothgar's counsellor. See 499n.
URSULA The name given to Healfdene's daughter, Onela's wife. 61n.

WÆLS Father of Sigemund.
WAYLAND The smith of the gods, the northern Vulcan.
WAYMUNDINGS The family of Wiglaf, Weoxstan and Beowulf. See
    2593n.

READ MORE IN PENGUIN

In every corner of the world, on every subject under the sun, Penguin represents quality and variety – the very best in publishing today.

For complete information about books available from Penguin – including Puffins, Penguin Classics and Arkana – and how to order them, write to us at the appropriate address below. Please note that for copyright reasons the selection of books varies from country to country.

In the United Kingdom: Please write to *Dept. EP, Penguin Books Ltd, Bath Road, Harmondsworth, West Drayton, Middlesex UB7 0DA*

In the United States: Please write to *Consumer Services, Penguin Putnam Inc., 405 Murray Hill Parkway, East Rutherford, New Jersey 07073-2136.* VISA and MasterCard holders call 1-800-631-8571 to order Penguin titles

In Canada: Please write to *Penguin Books Canada Ltd, 10 Alcorn Avenue, Suite 300, Toronto, Ontario M4V 3B2*

In Australia: Please write to *Penguin Books Australia Ltd, 487 Maroondah Highway, Ringwood, Victoria 3134*

In New Zealand: Please write to *Penguin Books (NZ) Ltd, Private Bag 102902, North Shore Mail Centre, Auckland 10*

In India: Please write to *Penguin Books India Pvt Ltd, 11 Community Centre, Panchsheel Park, New Delhi 110017*

In the Netherlands: Please write to *Penguin Books Netherlands bv, Postbus 3507, NL-1001 AH Amsterdam*

In Germany: Please write to *Penguin Books Deutschland GmbH, Metzlerstrasse 26, 60594 Frankfurt am Main*

In Spain: Please write to *Penguin Books S. A., Bravo Murillo 19, 1°B, 28015 Madrid*

In Italy: Please write to *Penguin Italia s.r.l., Via Vittorio Emanuele 45/a, 20094 Corsico, Milano*

In France: Please write to *Penguin France, 12, Rue Prosper Ferradou, 31700 Blagnac*

In Japan: Please write to *Penguin Books Japan Ltd, Iidabashi KM-Bldg, 2-23-9 Koraku, Bunkyo-Ku, Tokyo 112-0004*

In South Africa: Please write to *Penguin Books South Africa (Pty) Ltd, P.O. Box 751093, Gardenview, 2047 Johannesburg*

READ MORE IN PENGUIN

Beowulf: A Glossed Text
Edited with an Introduction, Glossary and Notes by Michael Alexander

The Anglo-Saxon poem *Beowulf* marks the beginning of English literature.

Eighth-century in origin, composed to be recited aloud, it told its Anglo-Saxon listeners a story of their Scandinavian ancestors. It celebrates the hero Beowulf, who goes to Denmark and slays the monster Grendel and Grendel's mother. He later becomes the king of Greatland, and in old age meets death in combat with a dragon. Blending history with legend and richly allusive in its narrative, *Beowulf* portrays an epic conflict of good and evil, generosity and vengeance, life and death.

In this new edition for the Penguin English Poets series, the Old English verse text is faced by a page on which almost every word is glossed. Michael Alexander provides full critical apparatus including notes, a map and an illuminating introduction to the poem and its provenance.

Revised 2000